Miss You Dad!

Story of a Father Beyond Courage

Ravi Sharma

INDIA • SINGAPORE • MALAYSIA

ISBN 979-8-89026-835-8

With love, Yashmit.

Disclaimer

The following storybook is based on an actual incident. However, the characters, their names and the incidents portrayed in this book are purely fictitious. Any resemblance to any person, living or dead, or any incident is purely coincidental.

The author of this book has no intention to hurt anyone's religious sentiments, any community, individual or country. The author has used creative liberty to portray the events and characters in this book and does not intend to offend anyone in any way.

The storybook is meant for entertainment and should not be taken as a reflection of reality. Any opinions or views expressed in the book are solely those of the author and do not represent the views of any organization, community or individual.

By reading this book, you acknowledge that the events and characters portrayed are fictitious and any resemblance to any person or incident is coincidental.

As quoted by the Author

जब तक मरे नहीं, ज़िंदा हो!

You Are Alive Until You Die!

With determination, there are no limits to what we can achieve.

A small, yet courageous creature can conquer even the tallest mountain or the fiercest animal.

The key is to believe in ourselves and our abilities and to be willing to take on challenges with a fearless spirit.

Remember that anything is possible when we have the courage and tenacity to pursue our dreams.

– Ravi Sharma

It is a difficult truth that sometimes, an event or a person can come into our lives and completely turn them upside down. For me, that is exactly what happened. It felt like my world had been destroyed, leaving me with nothing but pain and heartache.

At the right time, when that person gets immense pain, it relieves our wounds. Their painful screams and yearning bring comfort to our hearts.

I am enjoying the same peace today.

The scene in the dark and musty room was harrowing. With a strong hammer in hand, I relentlessly attacked him, breaking all the nails on his hands and feet. Clutching my knife tightly, I kept a steady grip on his neck—my hand already drenched in his blood. His appearance worsened by the minute as I mercilessly slashed at him with all my might—deliberately avoiding his neck. I wanted him to suffer, to die a painful death—a desire my father had instilled in me.

As he moaned in agony, blood flowed from his body, staining the walls and everything around him. His screams echoed in the room but I was immune to them. Was it sorrow or my passion for revenge that made his cries fall on deaf ears? In his teary and swollen eyes, there was a question that he asked in a groaning voice, "I treated you like my brother. Why are you doing this, Shahid?"

He lay on the ground, covered in blood, crawling towards me—pleading for mercy. "If you want to kill me, shoot me or slit my throat," he said and begged for death.

But I was determined to make him suffer until his last breath, as per my father's wish.

At that moment, my mind drifted to my father's favourite song by Kishore Kumar, and I began to sing it loudly as he continued to sob and cry.

Do not stop; you lose somewhere.

Shall go on thorns, Will meet the shadow of spring,

Oh, Walker. Oh, Traveller. Oh, Walker. Oh, Traveller.

See, the sun has stopped, has bowed before you.

Now his screams had stopped. Death was gripping him in its lap.

Sitting in front of him, I was at immense peace—watching as his breathing became shallower with each passing moment. It was clear that he was on the brink of death but somehow, he kept holding on…perhaps wanting to know who I was and why I was killing him.

In the silence of the room, the blaring of police sirens grew louder and louder as they closed in on me. The door began to shake as they pounded on it—desperate to get inside.

Time was running out for us both.

I bent to my knees and whispered in his ear—in Mumbai on 26th November 2008—"Miss you, Dad."

As I spoke, his eyes widened in shock before he took his last breath.

The door to the room had been violently forced open, and the police began firing wildly in my direction.

In my last fleeting moments, I whispered through tears, "I'll miss you, Dad."

This is the story of my life—the tale of Avinash.

Mumbai, November 26th, 2009.

Contents

About the Author

Ravi Sharma, a multifaceted individual with a diverse background in management, information technology and education, and having over 18 years of experience in corporate relations, brand management, training and placements, has established himself as a well-known name in the education industry. He has been instrumental in shaping the careers of numerous students and young talent and has had a significant impact on their lives.

While Ravi's professional accomplishments are impressive, his creative side is equally noteworthy. He believes in the power of words and thinking, which has led him to embark on a new journey as an author. Ravi's imagination and brilliance have resulted in his debut book, **The Last Crystal Arrow**, which has been highly acclaimed by his readers. The book's theme, concept and story have struck a chord with many, and it has been received with much appreciation.

Ravi's next book, **Miss You Dad**, is a courageous attempt that presents a story never heard before. It is a heartfelt tribute to a father that explores the depths of a father-son relationship. Ravi's unique ability to weave stories that resonate with his readers is what sets him apart from other authors. His writing is engaging, thought-provoking and emotionally stirring.

In summary, Ravi Sharma is a successful professional, an accomplished educator, and a talented author. He has proven his mettle in various fields, and his creative pursuits have opened new doors of opportunities for him. With his literary endeavours, Ravi has become a respected figure in the literary world, and his works continue to inspire and move his readers.

Chapter 1

Banaras Dairy – Part 1

Banaras, the spiritual capital of India, dates to the 11th century BC.

It is a city of temples and people who have immense belief in the power of God, which makes it unique.

The people's unwavering faith here in Lord Shiva is the one belief that drives this city.

Poor God! People come to him with all kinds of requests. It can be for a job, a daughter's wedding in the wealthiest family, a government job for sons, a good score in an examination, exceptional growth in business, an international trip, impressing a girl or boy and whatnot.

The responsibility of fulfilling every wish lies with my God, Lord Shiva.

A devotee donates fruits, flowers, sweets, clothes and money to the temple towards a fee to fulfil his wish.

Still, the biggest challenge is to directly communicate our wishes and feelings to God—to convince him to accept our wishes, and the most vital medium was invented as the *priests*.

Do you know what this link is about? Trust!

Trust is a simple word but has a deep meaning and impact. A simple stone is worshipped like a God, and so is a man. People and things around us have been given the status of God because of people's faith.

Mother always used to say, trust yourself first because God is in us first. It would help if you believe in yourself—that nothing is impossible. Even a tiny ant can kill an elephant which is a thousand times bigger than itself. A person can cross the enormous seas and mountains with his courage. She always taught me never to let my confidence go down or to break someone's trust. Worship God daily, not out of fear but faith, because he always has a better plan for you.

Due to this, we speak our hearts out and bow down while joining hands before the supreme power and live with the belief that someone is looking after us.

I trust this universal power, but I never took the help of any connecting link between God and me. I mean, *priests*.

This was one of my most significant disputes with my father, Pandit Kripa Shankar Tripathi.

He was one of the most revered names amongst the priests of Banaras. Whatever the problem would be, he would always have a solution. As much as people believed in God, they used to believe in him because of his knowledge and solutions. He was a busy man with many people coming to him with their requests to convince God to grant their wishes.

I was proud of his recognition in the city and people visited him from across the state. But I never liked him playing with people's trust and sentiments for a few thousand.

I often heard him tell my mother that truth and honesty are perfect things but they do not run one's house. Every person must sacrifice either or both virtues at some point in life. If people come to me out of trust, seeking solutions, I try to reach out to God honestly with my knowledge.

But he understood neither his wife, Rukmani, nor Avinash, his younger son—neither was convinced.

In the difference between being wrong and right, I was standing far away, which kept increasing.

I was his worthless and weak son. We had minimal or negligible interaction.

No matter how long the branch of a tree is, it will always remain as a part of the tree and can never be separated. No matter how many disagreements we had, the silence between us held us together.

Apart from me, he also had another brave, loving, good-hearted and obedient son—my elder brother, Prakash. We were opposite to each other by nature. Prakash's personality was fickle, domineering and opportunistic. Confidence, courage, flattery and full of poise—that was him. He had already ventured into politics, was a good businessman and gradually gained many followers.

With each day that passed, he got more praise, popularity, success and power.

There is a close relationship between power and pride.

As power increases, so does pride. Slowly and gradually, this made Prakash a little clumsy.

Prakash was now called *the Big Brother of Banaras*!

My father was considered in high esteem and held high status as a renowned chief priest in the city. Seeing the success of his elder son, it had already become a matter of pride for him to see his son become so well-established as a youth icon and have an excellent reputation in society.

Prakash developed a vast youth following and his win in the forthcoming assembly elections was certain. He was deeply well-connected with influential people, prominent leaders and eminent government officials. He landed a helping hand with many and at a faster pace, grew enmity with many more. This is the bitter truth of politics. But he did not stop and went on.

Soon, he realized the importance of being powerful. Otherwise, his survival would have been difficult.

Prakash had a sensible and settled personality. He never intentionally tried to harm anyone. But he had chosen politics for his career, where neither one is a friend nor an enemy. Everyone looks for their benefits.

His motive was always to take people along. Many went with him, and a few against him. He worked hard, and a vast public opinion continuously joined in his support.

We both used to talk very little—maybe once or twice a month—maybe only when he wanted me to do something or when I would run out of money. He always kept him busy with his work and he rarely stayed at home.

There was so much that he did not know about me which I wanted him to.

I wanted him to know that I felt really alone and missed Mother every day.

I could not speak or express myself to my father—out of fear.

Like any other boy, I always looked for my brother's support if I was harassed, scared and threatened by others.

I often realized that my father could very well sense and understand all that I was going through but he did not lend me his supporting hand. His entire focus was only on Prakash, of whom he was incredibly proud.

After all, why not? I was always considered to be his weak and useless son.

Anyone could threaten, bully or make fun of me. Initially, in school, and now in college and the locality, people bothered me without any reason. They used to make fun of my speech and personality. A few had immense sympathy for me and considered me to be a simple boy. For many, I was no less than an idiot.

But why was I tolerating all this? Was I a coward?

No, I was not. I lacked courage and needed someone to tap my shoulder and say, "Come on, get up and stand for yourself."

Mother, where have you gone…leaving me all alone? You were my greatest strength.

She passed away five years ago. I had a lot to say and learn from her but it could not happen. Whenever I was worried and scared, I ran to her. She would pacify me with her affection. My tears, troubles and fears have always been called cowardice by my father.

My brother, Prakash was 11 years older than me. Being small, I got more time, attention and love from my mother. She used to worship a lot and had great faith in God. Every night, she used to tell me a story before I went to sleep. Sometimes, she would narrate the story of the famous writer, Munshi Premchand or read stories about Akbar-Birbal, and many a time, tales of patriotism and freedom fighters. As I grew up, my mother's stories transformed into the sacred scripture of Hinduism. These three texts were the *Ramayana*, the *Mahabharata* and the *Bhagavad Gita*. These three holy scriptures taught me a lot about tolerance, love and gratitude towards others, the difference between right and wrong, self-confidence and when and how to fight for my rights.

Yes, I was neither weak nor cowardly. It was just because of my bravery and willpower that I endured whatever happened to me. I was left to learn from my mother—when to stand up and say, "Enough is enough!"

That scene from the hospital was still in front of me— when my father was running around and arranging money for my mother's treatment.

Perhaps, my mother knew that her time had come. She held both of our hands and said, "Lord Shri Ram and Lakshman felt unbreakable love and they supported each other in every odd situation. My two sons, Prakash and Avinash, will always be with each other—promise me."

Before we both could say anything, she had left us forever. Her hand's grip loosened but her eyes were wide open—as though she was waiting for our replies. We both looked at each other, hugged her and started crying. Father had also come. He closed our mother's eyes with his hand. We both could see the shame and self-humiliation on his face which showed that he could not afford good treatment for our mother due to the paucity of money. Like me, Dad and Prakash, too were deeply impacted because of my mother's death.

Prakash fulfilled his promise as he had given to our mother. He ensured that he fulfilled all my demands, needs and wishes. Our family became financially stable. We obtained great recognition and stature in society, and for every person who insulted and denied us help that day, they either approached us with their hands folded or could not look into my father's eyes in shame.

The reason was *Prakash.*

Prakash used to miss Mother very much but never revealed that fact to anyone. Often, I saw him looking at our mother's picture which was kept in the temple, for hours with moist eyes—thinking no one was watching him.

He knew that he was his father's greatest strength. He always carried himself with strength and determination. In fact, he was even braver than anyone else in the family— possessing strong willpower and exuding confidence. However, we both shared one common vulnerability—we would find ourselves weeping alone while remembering Mother.

It was nearly two o'clock at night when Prakash returned home—which was not long ago. He went to the temple and stood before a picture of our mother.

Perhaps he had something to say but only tears flowed from his eyes.

Unable to hold back my emotions, I embraced him tightly from behind.

"Look, Mother, today, your son has finally expressed that he misses his brother. For so many years, he only kept listening to our conversations while hiding in the background," Prakash spoke with a heavy heart.

After who knows how many years, we hugged each other tightly. Both of us shed tears.

Prakash continued, "Mother, I have kept my promise—just as you taught me. I have been working hard with dedication and I will continue to do so. Our lives have improved significantly and there is no scarcity of anything. You were right about Father. He feels lonely after your departure. I believe I have been a good support to him—in striving to keep him happy. I genuinely try my best and will keep doing so."

"Your little boy, Avinash, is also doing well, Mother. I understand that he couldn't spend as much time with you as I did, and regrettably, I couldn't devote as much time to him as I would have liked. However, I am doing my utmost to ensure that he lacks nothing and can lead a comfortable life. But there's one thing I will never be able to do—he misses you deeply, and I can never fill this void in his heart."

"You know, Mother, your younger son is about to graduate, and I will make sure he studies as much as he desires. Your elder son has become a successful businessman, and with your blessings, he will soon embark on his political journey. Dad is doing well and both of us promise to take care of him constantly."

"Dearest Mother, I will never forget you. Your absence is felt every single moment, even amidst all the happiness around," Prakash said—his eyes glistening with tears, as he held my hand and looked at our mother's picture.

Although we boys appeared to be strong, the truth was that we were quite vulnerable and weak at times. Like anyone else, we too needed support in our lives and it could come from anyone. Now, if I were to tell you that my mother is still with me and I can see her, you might think that I'm crazy. However, it is the absolute truth. She is with me, much like my shadow. Whenever I find myself feeling confused, alone, disappointed, upset or feeling helpless, she always seems to come and embrace me— providing the comfort and solace that I need.

That day, I realized that Prakash was profoundly lonely. For countless years, he toiled tirelessly, day and night, ensuring a good life for us without ever asking for or saying anything.

I embraced him tightly, vowing to myself that I would forever be his shadow, just as Lakshman had been for Lord Ram—as our mother had instructed.

With tear-filled eyes, I held Prakash close but through my blurry vision, I saw someone else's face. I hastily wiped away my tears, and to my astonishment, it was our father!

I was taken aback and almost had a half-hearted shock. Something seemed amiss, as I witnessed him crying for the first time. Perhaps, he had been listening to our conversation. He hugged both of us, and tears flowed freely from his eyes too. For the first time in my life, my father kissed my forehead—it was a gesture filled with love and vulnerability. He said to us, "Your mother cannot come back now. Can your father fill the void left after her demise?"

That one night dissolved all the emotional distance between us.

The next day was a new dawn and a brand new beginning for us.

Everything had changed. My father dropped me off at college and jokingly said, "If anyone bothers you, just let me know, and I'll take care of them."

We both burst into laughter after sharing a light moment.

A beautiful phase was about to begin in Prakash's life. Someone new was slowly entering his world, and I only found out about it after returning from college.

Another notable figure in Banaras was the renowned lawyer, Sonali Choudhary. She possessed incredible beauty, intelligence and brilliant legal knowledge. At the district court of Varanasi, she was famously known as the *lioness lawyer* due to her unmatched prowess in arguing during cases, crafting clever legal drafts and presenting her cases with the most relevant references. It was no surprise that she was highly esteemed amongst the judges in that court.

Little did I know that she was going to be my future sister-in-law. Prakash was one of her clients, who often sought her counsel for business matters and political and legal advice. Unbeknownst to her, she had gradually given her heart to her client, and her biggest dilemma was how to approach that situation while staying true to her professional responsibilities.

If that had been a courtroom case, she would have already emerged victorious. However, it was a matter of love, and she had to knock on the door of a different court—the one famously called the heart, specifically, Prakash's heart.

Although she was undoubtedly fearless in many aspects, when it came to matters of the heart, she carried a fear of the unknown. Love, with all its beauty, makes a person incredibly precious and significant in one's life. The mere thought of living without someone brings forth the fear of losing him or her, whether he or she is with someone or not. Love and anxiety share an intricate and profound relationship, and often, we find the strength to overcome our fears by embracing love and holding onto it with all our might.

As per our usual routine, my friends and I stopped at our favourite sweets shop for tea and *samosas*. Just as I took a bite, a beautiful voice reached my ears, and asked, "Are you Avinash?"

Turning around, I beheld a stunning woman with a delightful smile on her face. Now, two dilemmas presented themselves. Firstly, a bolt of excitement surged through my body. It was the first time a woman had addressed me by my name, and her voice sounded so lovely. Usually, everyone simply called me *brother, brother and brother.*

In a fleeting moment, happiness turned into nervousness, and I hurriedly swallowed the bite, realizing that before me, stood a lady who was a lawyer in her uniform. The only difficult question in my mind was, *what had I done?*

She smiled and asked again, "You are Avinash, right?"

I replied, nodding in affirmation, "Yes."

In a nervous voice, I asked, "Who are you?"

She calmly replied, "I am Sonali."

Before I could say anything else, she said, "Order tea and *samosas* for me as well. We need to talk."

My friend, Govind, promptly placed the order—that cheeky guy! He whispered in my ear, "Bro, lucky you!"

"Why are you late today? I've been waiting for you for the last 30 minutes!" Sonali remarked.

I glanced at my friends, who were staring at me with wide, open eyes.

Summoning some courage, I responded, "I'm sorry, I am not interested, and I don't even know you. Can you please leave?"

She replied with an understanding tone, "That's okay, little brother."

Oh, Lord, will every girl call me brother? I thought but at that moment, my primary concern was preserving my good reputation in front of my friends.

"Okay, fine, tell me, what is it all about? Yes, I am Avinash. Please tell me how I can help you," I said firmly.

"Prakash always told me that his brother, Avinash is very simple, intelligent and has a calm personality. But you seem to be an angry young boy too," Sonali said with a smile, her eyes becoming moist.

"I was busy figuring out whether what I'm doing is correct or not. I probably don't have any other option as your brother is not answering my calls or messages. Even for work, he sends his assistants," Sonali explained.

By then, I understood that it was a serious matter. At the same time, I felt angry with Prakash's behaviour. How could anyone break the heart of such a lovely woman?

"This may not be the right place to talk. If you'd like, can we talk while we walk? My house is nearby," I suggested.

"I know your house is nearby," Sonali replied.

I chuckled and said, "Well, you have done a thorough investigation of your case."

Blushing, she responded, "Shut up."

We started talking as we walked and she conveyed everything without even saying a word. It felt as though my mom was with me—guiding me and explaining something important.

I realized a few things that day. Everyone needs a life partner who understands and loves them unconditionally. No matter how much fear, pride or ego we carry in our hearts, it should never hinder our relationships. Expressing our feelings is essential. We must give ourselves a chance, regardless of the outcome.

I was not sure if Sonali had expressed her love for Prakash but I was delighted to know that someone loved him deeply—which he desperately needed. After meeting her for the first time, I could not comprehend why she chose to talk to me but I was genuinely happy for him and hoped that they would be together.

I knew Prakash well. I understood him deeply. He had his fears and a tendency to be afraid of happiness.

"We should strive to make the right decisions in life and leave the rest to God, as He always has the best plans for us. Can you please hand over this envelope to him?"

I extend my hand fearlessly with full faith and honesty.

"He should also do the same—believing that I am always with him. There is nothing bigger than faith in our lives."

"Mom used to say the same, didn't she?" Sonali remarked before leaving.

That day, I saw my mother too. She was standing at the door of the house, smiling—as if she had already accepted Sonali as Prakash's wife and her daughter-in-law.

As evening approached, I eagerly awaited Prakash's return. After all, happiness was about to grace our house, like the much-needed rain after a long wait.

Late at night, Prakash finally arrived home. I rushed to his room and stood at the door. He looked at me and said warmly, "Why are you standing there? Come here!"

I asked, "Should I make tea, or would you like to have dinner?"

As he switched on the TV, he glanced at me and asked, "Do you want to talk about something?"

"Yes," I replied curiously.

"Is Dad asleep?"

"Yes, but should I call him too?" I asked excitedly.

Prakash emphasized the point, "What's the matter, Avinash? Do you want to call our father to discuss something?"

"My graduation is about to be completed, and I am considering enrolling in an MBA programme," I disclosed.

"That's good! Have you thought about any college?" he asked eagerly.

"Yes, I have a couple in mind but the fees are quite high. Additionally, the cost of my stay and daily expenses is also a concern," I admitted hesitantly.

Prakash came over to me. Placing his hand gently on my head, he said, "Don't worry about it. I'll take care of everything. You just need to prepare and study well."

"You know, Avinash, there is so much that I couldn't accomplish, and I hope and wish for you to achieve it all. You should venture out, explore the world and share many stories with me that I will cherish for the rest of my life. I am already proud of you, my little brother, and I always will be."

He gazed at me as if seeking a commitment from my side. I nodded in agreement with his heartfelt words.

Seeing my eyes moisten, he asked, "Is there something else?"

"Can I ask you one thing?" I said, holding Prakash's hand.

"Sure," he replied.

"Would you never do anything for yourself?" I asked him.

Prakash looked at me in surprise and questioned, "Why do you say that and what does that mean?"

I responded, "You seem to dedicate yourself entirely to others—always putting their needs above your own. But what about your desires and dreams?"

He paused for a moment and then replied, "What more could I possibly need? I am already a distinguished youth leader and a successful businessman. I have a loving father and you, who care for me deeply. What else could I possibly want?"

I gently probed, "How about finding someone special with whom you can share all your fears and talk heart-to-heart?"

At that moment, I handed him an envelope—my hands trembled with fear. "I may be much younger than you, Brother, but I just want to say that we shouldn't let the fear of losing happiness keep us from pursuing it. I don't know what Sonali has written in this letter but please read it once. Maybe Mom wants the same."

As he took the envelope from me, a mix of emotions filled the room, and we both anxiously awaited his reaction.

I left the envelope carefully on Prakash's bed, and as I walked out of the room, his eyes followed me. I chose not to turn back, leaving him to discover the letter on his own.

That day, something remarkable happened. Prakash finally received the love and understanding that he had longed for in his life. He seemed genuinely happy with a newfound sparkle in his eyes and a willingness to embrace a fresh start and a better life.

Before I continue with the story, let me ask—did you know that Banaras is the only place where people also bless God? It is true!

The next morning brought a sense of renewal. The day was filled with happiness, music and a big smile adorning Prakash's face. It was around 8 a.m., and the melodious tunes emanating from Prakash's room spread joy throughout the house.

As I was also getting ready for college early that morning, I noticed Prakash was exceptionally well-dressed and seemed ready to leave. He was humming a cheerful tune, exuding positive energy.

Our father inquired, "You got ready quite early today. Are you going somewhere?"

"Yes, I need to go to the court. Some important papers need to be taken care of, and the elections are about to begin," Prakash replied, looking at me with a smile and a wink.

He appeared to be in a hurry, and our father insisted, "Hey, have your breakfast before you leave."

Prakash declined politely, "I'll have it there. Please, both of you, have it."

With that, he left for his destination. Meanwhile, I walked towards my college with a joyful heart, anticipating a day filled with fun and excitement. As I strolled along, I noticed a saint passing by Lord Shiva's temple. He paused for a moment and blessed the deity, saying aloud, "Stay happy always and keep living."

The positive energy seemed to be flowing all around, filling the day with a sense of optimism and hope. Little did I know what the future held for Prakash and the path that lay ahead for him.

I, too, was brimming with joy and fun as I continued my walk but then, I stopped in front of the temple and spontaneously began to bless God. "Keep on living, stay happy, have fun and all good things!" I exclaimed with genuine enthusiasm. The priest of the temple could not help but burst into laughter upon seeing my exuberant display.

Days passed, and then months. Life was going well. Prakash and Sonali were pleased but her brother, Bhairav Chaudhary, did not like him.

It was an intense and terrible political enmity, which Bhairav wanted to win at all costs. Only one man could help him—Mohammad Ilyas Rizvi, a contender for the councillor post. Rizvi had a well-established construction business, even though he was doing more illegal work under the guise of that business. It was known to everyone but as he was deeply rooted in various political and influential sources, no action was ever taken against him. Knowingly or unknowingly, Prakash had become a threat to him, and one of the goals of this highly vocal election agenda was to create a *crime and felony-free state*. For him, losing the election was the biggest threat.

Rizvi had an additional reason to harbour animosity towards Prakash—his deep attraction to Sonali. Despite already being married and having three children, Rizvi's desire to marry her persisted. Bhairav was well aware of Rizvi's infatuation and cunningly exploited it to further his political ambitions. He struck a dark deal with Rizvi by offering his support in winning the election in exchange for Rizvi's cooperation. The agreement included getting Sonali to marry Rizvi and providing assistance in his illicit activities.

Bhairav, driven by a desire for power and influence, saw this alliance with Rizvi as a means to consolidate his political career. He was willing to manipulate and exploit the situation to achieve his objectives, regardless of the harm it could cause to others, including his sister, Sonali.

As the political game unfolded, Sonali remained unaware of the sinister plot that was being woven behind the scenes. Little did she know that her happiness and future were being traded as pawns in a dangerous game of ambition and deception.

Is winning by any means or at any cost so crucial that we even forget humanity? Perhaps this is another disgusting face of politics.

We were all unaware of this. Prakash's election campaign was going on in full swing. We were all happy and were sure that he would win.

Gradually, happiness began to grace our household, one event at a time. Firstly, I received the delightful news of my admission to the University of Mumbai for a management programme, which filled me with joy and anticipation. Next, another reason to rejoice came with Prakash and Sonali's engagement. Their love blossomed, and they decided to take their relationship to the next level.

Sonali's father, feeling thrilled with their commitment, wished to celebrate their marriage with grandeur and festivity. He planned for the wedding to take place right after Prakash emerged victorious in the elections. The prospect of their union and the celebration of their love made our home brim with excitement and happiness. The anticipation of these upcoming events brought a sense of joy that filled our hearts, one beautiful moment at a time. Finally, the long-awaited day arrived—the elections were held, and Prakash emerged victorious with a resounding majority. The joy and elation in our father's heart knew no bounds. However, the happiness multiplied exponentially when Prakash's exceptional performance led to him being appointed as the cabinet minister for Finance and Parliamentary Affairs.

11th March 2000.

The day of Prakash's swearing-in ceremony had arrived, and the clock struck 8:00 a.m. Our home was filled with a joyful gathering of close relatives and enthusiastic supporters—creating a bustling and lively atmosphere. The air was charged with happiness and excitement, thus spreading a sense of joy all around us.

Our father had meticulously arranged for a bandwagon, which stood proudly at the entrance of the house. He looked resplendent in a bright white *kurta pyjama*—all ready to accompany Prakash to the oath-taking ceremony. With a heart full of pride, he held his head high and displayed a beautiful smile on his face. His happiness and contentment were evident to all, as he eagerly awaited the momentous occasion.

As the time approached for Prakash to take his oath, the anticipation and enthusiasm amongst the gathered crowd grew even more. It was a day of celebration, marking both Prakash's victory in the elections and the beginning of a new chapter in his political journey. The sight of our father's beaming smile and the joyous ambience around us made it a truly memorable and heart-warming moment for our family and everyone present.

Life is a remarkably strange journey. It can transform in the blink of an eye, without warning. No one can predict when, how or why these changes occur. Perhaps that's one of the reasons why we instinctively bow our heads and clasp our hands together in prayer before God, seeking His continuous blessings and guidance.

Not a single day had gone by when Prakash left the house without seeking the blessings of God and Mom. True to his routine, on that significant day, he sought divine blessings before proceeding to the ceremony. Sonali, too, stood at the main entrance of the house, ready to perform the sacred ritual. My father and I stood beside her, sharing the reverence and excitement of the moment.

The air was charged with a mix of emotions—hope, joy and a touch of apprehension. It was a pivotal day, marking the start of a new phase in Prakash's life. As he prepared to take his oath and embrace his responsibilities, the presence of loved ones and the act of seeking blessings added a sense of support and spiritual significance to the occasion. In those moments of transition and uncertainty, we found solace in our faith—trusting that God's blessings would guide and protect Prakash in his endeavours.

She had just finished performing the ritual, and as she prepared to apply the saffron on Prakash's forehead, a sudden and horrifying tragedy unfolded. In a heart-wrenching turn of events, a bullet pierced his forehead, thus tearing his head. The once joyous atmosphere turned into an eerie silence filled with shock and disbelief.

The devastating impact caused Prakash's blood to splatter on Sonali's face, and even our father's pristine white *kurta* was stained red with his blood. Prakash's lifeless body fell to the ground, and it became painfully evident that he was gone—leaving us all in a state of profound grief and sorrow.

The scene that followed was of chaos and despair, as the sound of screams and cries filled the air, and people began to panic and scatter in fear. Amidst the turmoil, my senses seemed to shut down, and my ears were numbed by the overwhelming shock.

Amidst that tragedy, Sonali's agonizing scream pierced the silence—expressing the magnitude of the loss and pain we were all experiencing. Our father, unable to fathom the reality before him, remained on his knees—gazing at Prakash's lifeless form in a state of disbelief.

In an instant, everything we cherished and held dear was shattered, leaving us with a void that could never be filled. Happiness had been cruelly snatched away and was replaced by mourning and devastation.

The tragic turn of events left us stunned and broken, forever altering the course of our lives. The memory of that fateful moment would forever haunt our hearts—reminding us of the fragility of life and the unpredictable nature of fate.

"Why, God? Why?" I cried out in anguish, unable to comprehend the cruel twist of fate that had befallen us.

Sonali and I clung to Prakash's lifeless body with tears flowing uncontrollably as we grieved like lost souls—overwhelmed with pain and sorrow.

After some time, the police arrived and took possession of Prakash's body for a post-mortem examination. The solemn moment served as a harsh reminder of the grim reality that we faced. Our world had turned upside down, and the emptiness left behind by Prakash's sudden departure felt insurmountable.

As the authorities carried out their duties, we stood there, numb with shock and disbelief—grappling with the void that was now a permanent part of our lives. The pain seemed unbearable, and the questions of *why* lingered— echoing in our hearts with no answers in sight. The tragedy left us shattered and forever changed with a profound sense of loss that would stay with us for the rest of our days.

"Go with your brother, Avinash. He is alone. Bring him back with you at the earliest," Father urged, his voice trembling with emotion. "Be with him—hold him tight."

Amidst the overwhelming haze of grief, I found it difficult to grasp the situation. My body felt like a lifeless stone, rendering me unable to move or make sense of the tragedy that had unfolded before us.

Sonali, ever compassionate, gently wiped my tears away and spoke with conviction, "Let's go, Avinash. We cannot leave him alone. Dad is right."

After what seemed like an eternity, we finally received Prakash's lifeless body, six hours after the heart-wrenching incident. With heavy hearts, we carried him in the ambulance and slowly made our way back to our home.

Upon our return, we found our father still sitting at the entrance of the house, where the light had cast its mark after Prakash's untimely demise. The sight of his grief-stricken form was heartrending, and I spoke to him with a voice laden with pain, "I have come, Dad."

He looked at me and said, "Let your brother be in the courtyard. Today is his last night in this house. Wait, I will come with you. How much will you do alone?" Father said while getting up.

With staggering steps, he started walking inside the house. He poured a bucket of water into the middle of the courtyard and sitting down on his knees, he started cleaning the floor with a cloth.

He looked at me angrily and said, "Why are you standing? Go get your brother quickly! Haven't I told you? Don't leave him alone! Go fast!"

I ran to the ambulance, crying.

As the news of the tragedy spread, a crowd began to gather outside our house, drawn by the heart-breaking incident that had befallen our family.

With Sonali's and my friends' support, we carefully brought Prakash's lifeless body to the courtyard. Until then, our father had not laid a fresh white cloth on the ground.

He gently spoke, "Let him rest here now. Be careful that he is not harmed. He is still my brave child!"

Hearing my father's words, I burst into tears.

Father lit a lamp and kept it on one side of Prakash's head. He sat beside him.

Sonali sat near Prakash's feet—her eyes filled with tears as she gazed at him intently. Her eyes seemed to hold numerous unspoken questions—seeking answers from Prakash, even in his lifeless state. Perhaps there were things left unsaid, feelings left unexpressed or memories that she wished to cherish forever.

With a trembling hand, she placed a letter in Prakash's pocket, as if leaving a part of her heart with him. In a whisper, she spoke into his ear, sharing her deepest emotions and bidding a heartfelt farewell. It was as if she wanted him to know that her love and devotion would forever be with him, even in the realm beyond.

With a sense of reverence, Sonali reached out and gently touched Prakash's feet, as if seeking his blessings for the journey that lay ahead for both. It was a poignant moment of love, respect and acceptance, as she embraced the reality of his absence but also embraced the everlasting bond that they shared.

Amidst the sea of sorrow and remembrance, Sonali's act of placing the letter and seeking Prakash's blessings spoke volumes about the depth of their connection and the beautiful memories that they had shared. In that quiet exchange, she found solace in the belief that their love would endure everything beyond that moment, carrying their bond into eternity.

Relatives, neighbours and well-wishers gathered to offer their final respects and pay homage to Prakash. The atmosphere was filled with an overwhelming sense of sorrow, and it was a day unlike any other I had experienced before.

Amongst the mourners, I saw my mother. Her tears mirrored the pain and grief that enveloped us all. As a mother, she had come to bid farewell to her beloved son, and her heartache was palpable.

As the night slowly passed, morning arrived but the darkness of grief still enveloped us all. It felt as if our sun had set, leaving us in a perpetual state of mourning.

Our father rose from his seat with a heavy heart and made his way towards Prakash's room. When he returned, he carried Prakash's beloved safari suit, watch and shoes—

the precious possessions that held a deep significance in Prakash's life.

With a tender gesture, our father placed all those cherished items in my lap and gently said, "Give your brother a bath and get him ready."

In that solemn moment, it was as if our father entrusted me with the responsibility of preparing Prakash for his final journey. With a mix of sorrow and reverence, I fulfilled his wishes—ensuring that Prakash would be presented with utmost dignity and respect.

As the news of Prakash's passing spread, thousands of his devoted followers arrived to bid him a final farewell. The sight of the crowd united in their grief and admiration for Prakash, served as a testament to the impact he had on countless lives.

Whispers spread amongst everyone—carrying the unsettling news that Mohammad Ilyas Rizvi was allegedly responsible for Prakash's murder, and Bhairav had supposedly conspired with him.

The most significant burden in this world is witnessing a father carrying his son's lifeless body. In that heart-breaking moment, one could see how shattered he felt inside, yet he refrained from shedding tears.

The weight of such a loss is immeasurable, and the pain that a father experiences when he has to bid farewell to his child is beyond description. It is a burden that no parent should ever have to bear, and yet, tragically, it is a reality that some have to face.

Dad was broken inside, but he stood firm.

The sorrow of losing someone you deeply love and have high hopes for in the future is indescribable. It is at that very moment when life seems to shatter, come to a close and reach its end. Prakash's untimely passing not only took away our cherished hopes but also robbed our father of the pride and joy that he had in his beloved son. The magnitude of the pain he experienced went far beyond any words, and the depth of his grief was beyond measure.

That day, it was not only Prakash who got killed!

It was the murder of my father's hopes, Sonali's golden dreams of a beautiful life and my biggest strength and supporter.

What we carried on our shoulders that day was not just a dead body but our lives. Slowly, we moved ahead towards the cemetery to burn the body into ashes.

Prakash was waiting for his final farewell and to be laid on the pyre.

The priests' *mantras* resonated in the ghastly silence.

Many people had come to pay homage and get the last glimpse of Prakash's body.

The presence of Mohammad Ilyas Rizvi at that moment was a perplexing and unsettling sight. His calm demeanour seemed to seep into my eyes—leaving me feeling poisoned by his apparent indifference. The mask of pretence he wore was evident to all, and it only added to the disgust that many, including myself, felt upon witnessing him there.

While others around me looked at him with disdain, there was an underlying fear that held them back from voicing their thoughts. However, I could not accept remaining silent in the face of such injustice. My heart pounded with an unexpected surge of courage, and my steps were on the verge of moving towards him.

"Perform the final rites of your brother, Avinash," Father solemnly instructed.

I stopped and could not move any further.

The very next moment made me feel weak—very weak.

He joined his hands in request and said, "I have lost one son but now, I do not dare to lose the other. The one with whom you now want to get involved is far away from all our grasp. I know that he is the reason behind Prakash's death. Let it be, my son," our father said and started crying bitterly.

The priests recited the *mantras* again, and I started squeezing sandalwood sticks into Prakash's pyre. It is said that the one who goes should be freed from all forms of love and emotions. Otherwise, his soul wanders.

Dad said, "Take that letter out of Prakash's pocket."

It was the letter that Sonali had kept inside his pocket. The message that was written was:

Listen, we will never pretend to love one another. We will not tell people how much we love each other.

Whenever I need you, please come and hold me, as always.

I will never let you be alone. I will always be your shadow.

Don't forget my daily hug and remind me how beautiful I look!

Do you know what, Prakash? You are my best and lifelong blessing from God!

Listen, never leave me, please. Our baby will need both of us!

Laughing, smiling, humming—this is how my life will pass!

Yours always, Sonali.

How strong was her love and how determined she was, I realized.

Oh, Prakash, why did this happen to you? You are so lucky, my brother. You have someone who loves you so very much, I thought.

This is the power of true love. Whether the one we love is with us or not, we love them, live every moment and design our beautiful worlds, either with or without them.

I lit the fire to ignite Prakash's pyre. Sonali kept looking at it with tears in her eyes and had a little smile on her face. It was certainly not the end but a new beginning for her.

Anyone who saw that was astonished but I knew that she had set out on a new journey of life with Prakash.

Slowly, people started leaving the crematorium. Sonali, Dad and I were still there, looking at Prakash's pyre.

He had gone away—far away. Only his memories were left, and we needed to live by them.

"You were my bright, intelligent and brave child. You have given me many such moments that I will always be proud of. You missed your mother a lot, didn't you? Now go to her and take all the love of your share," our father said with folded hands as he stood before Prakash's pyre.

Holding my hand, Father instructed, "Now take me home, Avinash. I am tired."

"Yes, Father," I replied, crying, and we left for home.

We had just reached home.

"Where are you going? What is left for you in this house? Let's go home, Sonali," Bhairav called Sonali.

Sonali turned and looked at him but she did not say anything. She kept moving inside the house.

Bhairav tightly gripped her hand and demanded, "Haven't you heard me? Come back home! Enough of your stubbornness and our parents' interference! Whatever may have happened in the past is done—you have no reason to be here now, and you no longer have any ties with this family," Bhairav growled—his voice filled with anger and frustration.

"Take care of your affairs, Bhairav. I don't need your advice. I had hoped you wouldn't create a scene here. I will come home when I decide to, and besides, you never accepted this relationship. I have never meddled in your life, and it would be better for you not to interfere with mine. You can leave now," Sonali asserted firmly, her voice unwavering and resolute.

"Am I the one making a scene? Me? Do you even know what the entire city is saying about you and our family? I'm telling you plainly and clearly—let's leave this place right now!" Bhairav retorted, his teeth gritted in frustration and anger.

"People are also talking about you and Rizvi…that you both…"

"Don't force me to say anything further! Just move from here, Now!"

"Is this the way to talk to your sister, Bhairav? Speak with love," said Rizvi, interrupting Bhairav.

"And don't get so angry, please. It doesn't suit your beauty, Ms. Sonali," Rizvi added with a cunning smile.

"I understand that you must be feeling incredibly low and devastated right now. I am no stranger to the pain of losing someone you love deeply. It's a sorrowful time but eventually, you must find the strength to move forward. Moreover, you have responsibilities towards your family that you can't ignore. Starting anew might be the best course for you, and if necessary, I'm willing to offer my support..." Rizvi's words trailed off as he attempted to place his hand on Sonali's shoulder but she immediately protested.

"Stay within your limits and don't you dare to cross your boundaries, Rizvi! I know you and everything about your evil intentions. And as far as my life is concerned, you have nothing to do with it. So why don't you just get lost too?" Sonali replied, warning Rizvi.

"Wow, that's truly astonishing. I can sense the immense love you have for me. It's probably one of the reasons why I'm so fond of you. But listen, my dear girl, you don't have the faintest idea about Rizvi. I always get what I desire, no matter the cost. Perhaps what you've heard from others may be true or false but the reality today is that we will be getting married very soon. And if you want, you can confirm it with your dear brother," Rizvi said with a threatening undertone, attempting to intimidate Sonali.

"Forget it, Rizvi. I will never belong to you, not in this lifetime or any other. Despicable individuals like you always stoop to such cheap tactics. But this time, you've messed with the wrong person. Let me make it crystal clear—Sonali was and will forever be devoted only to Prakash. As for moving forward in life, I already have—I moved forward with Prakash and our child," Sonali replied with unwavering resolve.

"Oh well, congratulations, Bhairav, you will be an uncle soon! But you never told me I would get a child for free with your sister," Rizvi said, making fun of Bhairav.

"This is dirty blood and a blot on our family, not my sister," Bhairav said.

Holding Sonali's hair firmly, Bhairav said, "Listen, abort this child, or else I will make your and your child's life hell. You will be married to Rizvi only, and this is final."

I charged at Bhairav, grabbed his neck and said, "How dare you abuse my brother, Bhairav!"

I charged at him, throwing punches as hard as I could. But Rizvi's strength proved overwhelming, and he retaliated with even greater force. Each blow he delivered hit me like a ferocious storm, knocking me to the ground.

As I lay defenceless, Rizvi's assault continued without mercy. He relentlessly kicked and punched me, causing pain to course through my entire body. Blood began to flow from my head, nose, and mouth, as my clothes were torn from the force of the attack.

Amidst the chaos, our father rushed to protect us but Bhairav, fuelled by anger, struck him as well, thus adding to the turmoil that engulfed us.

Sonali tried desperately to intervene and stop the violence with courage in her eyes but Rizvi seemed impervious to her pleas. He continued the assault without remorse, and with a sinister smile playing on his lips.

To our dismay, the people around us, including our neighbours and supposed supporters and followers of Prakash, merely stood as idle spectators. Despite their previous allegiance, no one came forward to help or intervene in the disturbing spectacle unfolding before them.

In that moment of distress and vulnerability, we felt abandoned and betrayed. The world seemed callous and indifferent, and justice appeared distant and unattainable.

Rizvi stood there, his smile a haunting reminder of the evil that lurked within him. The scene painted a grim picture of a world that had turned against us—leaving us to confront the harsh realities of a situation we never could have imagined.

That fateful day, I came to a stark realization—the world values power more than an individual's worth. Position and influence take precedence over the value of a person's life. Prakash's words rang true in my mind—having high stature and power is essential, for without it, this world will not allow you to survive.

Amidst the turmoil, we stood isolated and vulnerable, surrounded by threats and helplessness. The brutal encounter revealed the dark underbelly of a society that often places more significance on status and dominance rather than the well-being and dignity of human lives.

"I'm sparing your life for now. But make no mistake, if you ever dare to lay a hand on me again, I'll ensure that you suffer a fate worse than death, you wretched bastard," Bhairav declared with a menacing threat in his voice.

It appeared that someone had tipped off the police about the incident. However, upon their arrival, no action was taken against Rizvi and Bhairav, thanks to Rizvi's influential status. The police dismissed the matter as a family affair and left without conducting any inquiry or holding them accountable.

In a surprising turn of events, Police Inspector, Varun Pawar, who had always shown respect to my father, advised him to avoid causing any disturbance or uproar. It seemed that the times had changed, and even the police were hesitant to take action against influential individuals like Rizvi.

Undeterred, Bhairav tried to take Sonali with him but she firmly refused. With fierce determination in her eyes, Sonali slapped Bhairav and addressed him and Rizvi directly. She vowed to seek justice for Prakash, his family and herself by swearing upon his funeral pyre that they would be punished for their heinous deeds.

Sonali declared that her pursuit of justice would be a tribute to Prakash and their child. She firmly believed that the day they faced the consequences of their actions would be the day she would immerse Prakash's ashes, thus symbolizing closure and justice for the pain that they had caused.

In the face of adversity, Sonali's courage and conviction were unwavering. She was determined to fight for truth and justice, regardless of the obstacles in her path. Her words echoed the resilience of her spirit, vowing to never rest until justice was served for the injustices inflicted upon her loved ones.

"I promise that every day will be like a living hell. You will beg for mercy but you will not get it. You will cry every day but I will only bring you pain. You will find peace the day you surrender yourself to me," Rizvi said and was about to leave.

"It's a deal," Sonali replied.

My father and I were terrified after hearing those words from Rizvi but one thing about Sonali increased our courage—no one is bigger than the law—no one!

I do not know from where so much courage and faith came to her which could make both Father and me believe that Rizvi could not spoil anything for us.

Days, months and years passed by and Rizvi continued to haunt us.

The *Jan Samarthan* Party was the second-largest party after Prakash's republic party. With Rizvi's help, Bhairav became the Chief Minister. He, too, had left no stone unturned to wreak havoc on us.

Many a time, our house was pelted with stones—late at night. Quite often, our electricity was cut deliberately. Rizvi's goons used to set fire to our door by bursting liquor bottles.

I even stopped asking this question, "God, why? Why is this happening to us?"

Rizvi often harassed Sonali by passing cheap comments and dirty jokes, as well as by troubling her. But Sonali stood firm and kept fighting. She had filed a case against Bhairav and Rizvi for Prakash's murder. She kept fighting and battling but did not lose her courage.

All this went on and five months passed.

And one day…

"Is this where Avinash lives?" the postman asked and called out.

My admission letter arrived from the University of Mumbai.

The postman put the letter in my hand and said with a smile, "Not everyone gets admission to such a big university. Sweets will be required."

I gave him 10 rupees out of my pocket. He left happily.

But I just stood there and kept looking at that letter. It felt as though someone had buried my feet in the ground—I could not even move.

"What is it, Avinash? Why are you standing there? Come in," Dad asked.

I felt like I woke up from some deep sleep. There was a strange feeling of fear in my heart. I ran to my room and sat on the ground in one corner. The fingers of my hands were tightly clinging to that letter.

Dad came into the room and asked, "What happened? What's in your hand? Why are you so worried?"

Taking the letter from my hand, he tried reading it. "Mumbai…"

He could not read it well as it was in English. Expressing deep concern, he asked, "Do you plan to go to Mumbai—to become an actor?"

Our ears yearned to hear good news. "That's it, Father!" Sonali said and continued, "He wanted to study and got admission to the University of Mumbai."

"Get ready, Avinash. Move out of here. Move ahead in life and do something that will bring back the lost prestige of our family. This will be a reason for me and Dad to smile again and feel proud," Sonali said, making me understand the importance of the opportunity I had in hand.

"Prakash always wanted you to move out from here, do great in life, achieve success and show him the world. Don't lock yourself here. Look ahead and start now. Won't you fulfil his wish, Avinash?" Sonali added.

"Dad, can you please ask him to go? He needs to move out of here," Sonali said, crying.

"But how can I leave you and Dad like this here?" I replied worriedly.

"Move out from here and create your identity. It will make everyone happy here. Don't worry about Dad. I am here with him, always," she spoke.

Two days had gone by, and the time had come for me to depart from Varanasi. With a heavy heart, I sought the blessings of my father before stepping out of the house. As I stood at the threshold, ready to leave, he remained silent with his eyes fixed on me.

I glanced back one last time, and in his gaze, I sensed an unspoken message. His silence spoke volumes—it conveyed that he would undoubtedly feel the loneliness of my absence but he encouraged me to forge ahead in life and make a name for myself.

Though no words were exchanged, the depth of his love and support resonated with me. He wanted me to succeed, embrace new opportunities and build a future that would honour our family's values. I knew that his unwavering belief in me would be the guiding force as I embarked on a new chapter of my life.

With a heart filled with gratitude and determination, I bid farewell to the place that had been my home, knowing that my father's blessings would be a constant source of strength—propelling me forward towards my dreams and aspirations.

Sonali came to drop me off at the railway station.

"Please take great care of yourself! Continue to have regular check-ups with the doctor. It's only a few months before you become a mother, and happiness is about to grace our household. I am certain that this baby will bring new hope and joy to both you and Dad."

"You know, I always envisioned dancing in front of the mare—when you and Prakash were to be married—while I'd be welcoming my sister-in-law home. Though life took a different turn, I will still dance the day when this child enters the world because, on that day, it will feel as if Prakash has come back home too."

"Thank you from the bottom of my heart for loving him and everything you have done and continue to do for our family. Your courage and strength are admirable!" I expressed with folded hands, a smile on my lips, and tears of joy in my eyes.

Holding my folded hand, Sonali said, "You have brought your sister-in-law home, Avinash! I did what should have been the duty of a wife and daughter-in-law.

You are right. This baby is a new hope in my life—the return of happiness to our home—a reason for Prakash to smile—wherever he may be now."

The train's horn sounded loud.

"Now you go ahead…take care of yourself. Keep giving us an update about your life in Mumbai and study diligently. We will all wait for you."

"Always remember one thing, Avinash. No one can beat the one who makes a new beginning—even after everything is over," she spoke.

I touched her feet and stood at the door of the train.

The train had started, and Sonali kept looking, smiling and waving at me.

Some memories of relationships and some of my loved ones, I left.

With a broken, heavy heart, in the hope of finding a little peace, I left.

With a lot of unsaid words, I left.

Away from my city, my childhood, my home and my friends, in an attempt at a new life, I left.

Mom, Dad, Prakash and Sonali—I will miss you a lot!

Chapter 2

Mumbai Diaries

I do not recall when I fell asleep while lying on the berth. When I woke up and looked outside, I saw the signboard at Mumbai Central Station! The bustling city came into view—filled with a sea of people. The station was teeming with commuters, all in a hurry, rushing towards different destinations.

As I disembarked from the train, burdened by my heavy bags, I found myself amidst the chaotic crowd. Everyone seemed to be in a rush, and the frenetic energy of the city was palpable.

Suddenly, I collided with a man, and a brief moment of confusion ensued. He seemed visibly annoyed and questioned me, "Can't you see and walk properly?" I was unsure if he had bumped into me or vice versa but I quickly apologized and moved on, not wanting to escalate the situation.

Navigating through the throngs of people, I continued my journey, while marvelling at the vibrant and dynamic city that was presently my new home. Despite the initial encounter, I could not help but feel excited about the opportunities and adventures that awaited me in that bustling metropolis.

I had often heard that Mumbai was a city that could grant anyone's wishes if they had the right intent.

At that moment, all I wanted was to find a cab, and almost magically, my wish was immediately fulfilled. As I stepped out of the station, a vast row of Mumbai's famous yellow-black taxis came into view.

A hand grabbed my suitcase—scaring me—and asked, "Where do you want to go, Sir?"

Many people surrounded me. They were all taxi drivers. Before I could say anything, one pulled my suitcase and said, "Let's go, fast. I will take you to your destination for less money."

"Hey! Wait! Why are you pulling my stuff?" I asked and reacted. "I don't want to go. Leave my bag and go away, now!"

He gave me a strange look and in an irritated voice, replied, "So, are you here to stand all day and waste time? Nonsense! I don't know where they come from," he said and left.

Strange people, man! I said to myself but that kind of behaviour was insulting.

A scene from the actor Govinda's movie flashed in my mind—as soon as he came to Mumbai for the very first time, a thief ran away with his bag. Recalling all my movie experiences, I became extremely careful. Everyone was my suspect. I grabbed my suitcase tightly and moved ahead. Many taxis and the auto driver kept calling me—"Come here! Where do you want to go? I'll charge less, etc., etc."—and I kept moving forward.

I saw Mahadev, Lord Shiva. I mean, I viewed a taxi with a massive poster of Lord Shiva on the rear-view window. I quickly approached it and humbly asked, "Will you go to Mahatma Gandhi Road?"

That driver scanned me from top to bottom and asked, "It's a 10 km long journey by road. Where exactly do you want to go?"

"Oh, yeah, the University of Mumbai," I replied.

He gave me a strange look and asked, "It has eight gates. At which gate do you want to stop?"

"Okay, the main block's gate…one," I replied, smiling.

"You should have told me this before. You're wasting time unnecessarily," he remarked—staring at me.

Finally, I left for the university, and I gained two learning tips the moment I landed there—to be *precise* and *quick*!

Within only a few hours, I fell in love with the city.

My heart was happy and my mind was calm. The taxi's window was open. The cool breeze was singing a melodious song in my ears. I put my neck out the window and the wind kissed my forehead. It was truly a moment when I forgot all my sorrow.

A hoarding read, *Welcome to Mumbai!*

I shouted out loud, "Thank you!"

The driver asked with a smile, "Have you come to Mumbai for the first time?"

"How did you know?" I asked feeling surprised.

"I was happy the way you are, 10 years ago and I wanted to become a hero. Your appearance is good. You are smart with excellent features and your voice sounds impactful. Have you also come to become a hero?" he asked while he made fun of me.

"I did not come here to be a hero. But yes, one day—it will indeed happen—not only Mumbai but the whole world will be proud of me!" I said confidently.

"Dialogue! Dialogue!" the driver said and nodded.

What I said must have been like a joke to him but I had promised myself that I would be so successful that Prakash, Dad and Sonali would be proud of me.

I reached the university campus and completed the admission formalities. I was allotted a hostel and I checked into my room.

I had just entered the room and saw Lord Krishna. A boy was putting up a poster of Lord Krishna on the room's wall. Excellent! It was going well—first I saw Lord Shiva and then Lord Krishna—the day was full of blessings.

"Yes?" he asked with a smile.

"This is my room," I replied hesitantly.

"Hey, Tripathi *ji*, welcome," he said while he hugged me.

"I'm Suresh Kumar Yadav from Rewari, Haryana," he answered.

"And it's not yours, it's our room," he said and started laughing out loudly.

Isn't he too over-friendly? I said to myself, looking at him thoughtfully.

"What? What happened to you? Aren't you Avinash Tripathi? I am your roommate, buddy!" he said.

"Smile a bit. You are in the company of the Yadavs," he said and laughed loudly.

I began to settle in the room and adjusted my luggage and stuff.

"Can I take this side? I asked, pointing towards the left bed.

"And probably, if we can keep the beds along the wall for a good distance in between, the room will have an excellent moving space and will be comfortable as well," I added.

He came to me, put his hands on my shoulder and said, "Well, I was thinking whether we could join our beds and sleep together as I love sleeping with men. What do you think about this plan, my friend?"

He said that in a very serious and cheesy tone.

I took a step back and stood staring at him. He suppressed a smile, laughed and started jumping with joy across the room. "I was kidding," he replied, hugging me.

"Don't worry. You are in safe hands," he added with a laugh.

"You are, too," I replied and smiled. I welcomed my roommate with a hug.

We both helped each other in settling down in the room. Then we went for lunch and started to prepare for the very first day of college, which would be the next day!

He kept speaking, talking about himself, his family, Rewari, his girlfriend, oops, sorry, his girlfriends and whatnot.

I listened to him patiently and replied, " Okay, hmm, all right!"

I had enrolled in a management programme, but he was a tech guy. Thankfully we were only roommates but not batch mates. Else, it would have been difficult. But was I right in thinking so about him? I had to wait and see!

I wore a business suit for my first day at college, and for the first time in my life, I looked very smart. I got the suit stitched for Prakash's wedding. Anyhow, that day was my important day which he was also looking forward to.

I was equally irritated by Suresh, as he took exactly 45 minutes to bathe. I mean, who does that? And especially a man! I was running late and was feeling stressed and worried. It was a massive university complex, though, and with much difficulty, I finally reached the auditorium for the orientation programme.

It felt like a scene straight out of a Bollywood movie, just like Shahrukh Khan's grand entry in the movie *Kabhi Khushi Kabhi Gham*, where Jaya Bachchan was waiting for him at the gate. Similarly, as I arrived at the entrance, our Professor, Dr. Deepak Bagchi, welcomed me with warmth and enthusiasm. To my surprise, I was escorted to the stage and was accompanied by a few other students.

A wave of confusion washed over me. Why was I being led to the stage and asked to sit there? My mind raced with questions, and I could not help but wonder if it was because I had been the last student to enter the auditorium for the programme. Anxiety began to build within me, and I mentally prepared myself for a potentially embarrassing moment, fearing that I might face some kind of public reprimand.

At the podium, Dr. Bagchi, announced, "Well, my dear students, I am so excited to welcome our esteemed guests to the programme today. We are just waiting for the arrival of our esteemed dean, Dr. Shovandu Kalikoti, to begin the programme. Meanwhile, you all are suggested to put your mobile phones on the switched-off mode to ensure that no disturbance occurs during the ceremony."

"Oh no, what a misunderstanding!" I thought to myself. Looking around, it became evident that I was mistaken for a guest and not recognized as a fellow student. The reason behind the confusion was clear—I was the only one dressed in a business suit, while the rest of the students were casually clad in jeans, t-shirts and other relaxed attires.

I made several attempts to approach Dr. Bagchi and clarify the situation but he seemed preoccupied and did not provide me with an opportunity to explain. Every time I tried, he politely responded, "Sir, we apologize for the delay. The programme is about to begin. Please feel at ease."

I could not say anything.

Dean Dr. Kalikoti made his grand entrance into the ceremony area and was accompanied by a gentleman and he guided him to the dais. Taking the podium, he addressed the audience by saying, "Ladies and gentlemen, please join me in extending a warm welcome to a brilliant, young and exceptionally talented individual, one of the youngest entrepreneurs in India, Mr. Yashmit Sharma."

Dr. Kalikoti noticed my presence on the stage and exchanged a stern glance with Dr. Bagchi—indicating that I was not meant to be there. Realizing the gravity of the situation and not wanting to prolong the embarrassment, I quickly rushed towards Dr. Kalikoti and explained the misunderstanding.

I could not gauge his thoughts at that moment but he handled the situation with composure. He instructed me to return to the stage and stand in a corner—ensuring that I did not draw further attention to myself.

On the other hand, Dr. Bagchi's disapproval was palpable, and his gaze conveyed his frustration and anger towards me. I felt as if he had mentally condemned me many times over—wishing he could somehow make my embarrassment unbearable.

In that tense moment, it seemed like he wished to do away with me in the most drastic manner, expressing his frustration through vivid thoughts of harm that he would never actually act upon. The intensity of his disapproval made me feel like I was being judged relentlessly—as if I had committed an unforgivable mistake.

As I stood in the corner of the stage, I could not help but feel like an outcast amidst the ceremony that was supposed to celebrate achievements and talents. The humiliation weighed heavily on my heart, and I wished I could disappear from the spotlight and undo the unfortunate turn of events.

The programme began with ethnic lamp lighting and seeking blessings from Lord Ganesha. I was so impressed by the guest, Mr. Yashmit Sharma, the founder and CEO of Solutronix Systems, Asia's most promising chip-making company based in Bangalore. He was awarded the following titles—the Youngest Entrepreneur in India and the Top 10 in India by Forbes. He must have been about our age or a little older than us but was highly impressive. We had one similarity—I was smartly dressed—just like him.

Dr. Kalikoti was invited for his inaugural speech, and the moment he came to the podium, he said, "Students, you have enrolled in a management programme, and I must give you an essential piece of advice on your first day. Before anything, first, learn to manage yourself well. Please look at this gentleman standing opposite me. He is one amongst you, and how beautifully he has dressed today! This is the attire of a management professional."

"Gentleman, please come here and introduce yourself," he said, inviting me to the podium.

My heart was terrified, but that was my proud moment.

"Thank you so much, Sir for your kind words and recognition. My dear friends, I'm Avinash Tripathi from Varanasi. I feel pleased to be here in this esteemed institution," I said and settled amongst the other students in the audience.

The day went well. I sat next to someone throughout the day and never realized that I was being noticed.

As the days passed by, Suresh and I were having a good time together. My perception was continuously changing towards him. He was terrific with technology. He often demonstrated to me some excellent software interfaces he created himself.

Soon, It was Fresher's Day. I was getting ready for the event. Well, I had a dance performance for the very first time in my life.

My phone rang. It was a call from Sonali's number, but it was Dad on the call.

"Hello, Avinash, how are you doing? Where are you?" he asked in a low voice.

He seemed unnaturally calm.

"What happened, Dad? What's the matter? Are you okay, Dad?" I asked in a troubled voice.

"Yes, I brought Sonali to the hospital. I am here, alone. Everything is fine, don't worry, please. She needs to undergo an operation—it will be a Caesarean delivery. I hope you are not busy with your classes. Have I disturbed you, Son?" Dad asked.

"What are you saying, Dad? Not at all! Why didn't you inform me earlier? I would have come," I said, complaining all the while.

"It's not like I was concerned about your studies, and you shouldn't have come such a long way. I am here, don't worry. It's just that my age and health make me feel a little tired. I was a little worried and thought I'd speak to you," Dad said in a slow, low voice.

"Is her health fine? Are there any complications in the delivery?" I asked.

"She is fine. This brave girl was looking after herself during pregnancy—all by herself. I know everything will be okay. It's just that I don't trust my luck anymore. Happiness is around the corner after so much bad has happened to us. I am not used to happiness, which is why I feel scared. I do not have the courage left to see any sorrow," he spoke.

"I know, Dad. You are tired, feeling low and you've lost your confidence and courage. But it's not you who is weak. It was your time. You are and will always be the strongest. Now the bad time has passed, the tables have turned and it is smiling at you and all of us. Everything will be fine and good from now on," I said reassuringly.

"You have grown up, my child, and are wiser too. You are so mature that you can make your father feel better now. God bless you, my Son," Father said, laughing.

"I am fine. Now you do your work. I will call you as soon as the good news arrives," Father promised.

Oh, Almighty! May your blessings rain down upon us, I whispered in my heart. I fervently prayed for everything to go smoothly. Busily, I prepared for the awaited news while constantly checking my phone. The hours ticked by, from morning to afternoon, and then to evening, and as time passed, my concern grew.

The party had commenced, and the performances were underway. My group was scheduled as the third act to perform. I anxiously waited for Dad's call but it had yet to come.

As I stepped onto the stage, our dance performance had just begun. Suddenly, my phone vibrated. I had set it to silent mode to ensure that I would not miss Dad's call amidst the loud music. Despite the curious gazes from the audience, I promptly answered the call. It did not matter. My focus was on the call from my father.

I hastily answered the call and inquired, "Is everything alright, Dad?"

"Mother and Prakash have returned, Avinash!"

It was Sonali on the line, and her voice was filled with satisfaction, joy and happiness.

Despite the deafening music, every word from her reached my ears with crystal clarity—Mom and Prakash had returned.

"I've been blessed with twins—a boy and a girl. I was unconscious after the operation but I wanted to share this news with you personally. That's why I couldn't call earlier. Everything is fine. As soon as you can, please come home for a few days," Sonali earnestly requested.

Have you ever witnessed someone dance like a person possessed by pure joy? Have you seen someone throw all cares to the wind, and frolicking and dancing to the rhythm of their heart? That was precisely what I did that day. Uninhibited and carefree, my dance steps did not align or coordinate with those of my group members. Instead, I began celebrating a long-awaited moment that my family and I had patiently yearned for.

Tears welled up in my eyes, a radiant smile adorned my face and my heart overflowed with happiness. I danced with unbridled enthusiasm, unaffected by anything else happening around me.

Oh, indeed, my friends were not particularly pleased with my impromptu act. They believed that I had disrupted the entire performance. As we descended from the stage after our dance, I noticed the continuous gaze of disapproving eyes fixed upon me. Nevertheless, the show went on, and soon, all the performances concluded.

The Dean took the stage to announce the names of the two individuals who earned the coveted titles of Mr. and Ms. Fresher. Amidst the excitement, the party proceeded with a delightful dinner and a fantastic performance by the DJ. Despite the earlier incident, I did not let it dampen my spirits, and I thoroughly enjoyed myself throughout the rest of the event.

"I hope you are doing good and all right," someone spoke.

I had just picked up the dinner plate when that voice interrupted me.

I turned back, and a gorgeous woman was standing in anger.

"Are you alright? You seemed completely immersed in yourself—joyful, carefree and cheerful. It was a bit embarrassing for you and the group but it was genuinely heartening to witness your authenticity. Sometimes, it's crucial to be true to ourselves. Everyone is upset because you disrupted their dance performance but try not to be too hard on yourself. Just take it easy and chill," she said, trying to console me.

That person was Aditi Arora, my classmate, who had won the prestigious title of Ms. Fresher that evening. What was more, was that she held significant importance as she happened to be the daughter of one of the esteemed members of the college's board of advisers and, needless to say, a renowned businessman.

"Hi, I'm Aditi," she said while forwarding her hand for a handshake.

I replied hesitantly, "Who doesn't know you?"

"Oh, wow! Am I that famous? By the way, if you knew me, why didn't you talk to me or ask me out on a date?" she asked, smiling.

"Just like that," I replied, shyly.

Both of us started talking while the food was being served on our plates.

She gazed into my eyes, and a teasing smile played on her lips. She inquired, "Who called you during your performance that brought you so much delight? It seems like it was someone very special and important."

With joy and excitement in my voice, I replied, "Oh, yes! I'm incredibly happy today. Two little angels have arrived at my home. It was my sister-in-law informing me about her blessed twins. Our family had been eagerly awaiting this moment for a long time. I had been feeling so anxious since this morning, and when I received her call, I couldn't contain my happiness. I completely lost myself in the moment, danced like a madman, and ended up messing up the performance," I said, laughing, while tears welled up in my eyes.

"Oh, my goodness! What happened? Are you alright?" she asked with concern as she noticed my teary eyes.

"This is a moment of immense happiness. I'm sure your brother must be over the moon with excitement. He's truly fortunate. May God bless your entire family and the little ones," she said, and her excitement was evident as she laughed.

"You're absolutely right! It's such a fantastic occasion! Why are you still here? You must celebrate it with your family. Go home, meet everyone, have a fantastic party and cherish this special moment, my friend. Family is a precious gift and the greatest blessing. By the way, do you mind if I join you in your celebration?" she asked, reaching out to the waiter for two ice cream cups.

Raising the cups like a toast, she exclaimed, "Here's to you, your fortunate brother, your sister-in-law and the adorable little angels. Cheers to their good health, a wonderful life ahead and boundless happiness!"

She handed a cup to me.

I said, "Thank you" while I held the cup.

"I don't have a brother—he died last year. But I know that wherever he is now, he must be very happy today. Thank you so much, Aditi for making this moment special. I am truly honoured and touched," I said.

"Oh, I'm sorry, I didn't know that about your brother. Now I understand why your eyes were moist."

We both smiled and finished eating dinner.

"Well, you still need to answer my question. Why didn't you talk to me till today? she asked.

"Hmm, do you want me to be honest?" I asked.

"Yes, of course," she replied.

"I understand," I replied with a hint of self-consciousness. "I'm a bit reserved myself, and I never mustered the courage to approach you because of your aura. Being the daughter of such an influential person and a trustee of this university, as well as coming from a prominent family and growing up in a modern city like Mumbai, you exude an impressive presence—you're well-groomed, intelligent and beautiful. Why would someone like you talk to a guy like me? Many people wish to be your friends and have a conversation with you but they feel the same way. Just look around right now—many of my classmates are staring at me because I've been talking to you for so long," I chuckled, trying to lighten the mood.

"That's quite amusing, don't you think?" she said and responded cheerfully.

"I don't quite understand it either. Friendship is a matter of choice. It's not influenced by anyone's stature or status. In fact, I wanted to speak to you on our Orientation Day when everyone misunderstood you for the guest. But I hesitated. Seeing you on stage today—when you were full of excitement and joy and were fearlessly embracing the moment—was truly inspiring. It felt so lovely, and it motivated me to finally have this conversation with you today."

"You know, Avinash," she continued, "It's essential to cherish these small moments in life. They are incredibly precious, and no amount of stature or wealth can compare to their significance. Nothing is more valuable than being with family, friends and loved ones," she spoke with sincerity.

"You're absolutely right," she added thoughtfully. "Fame and wealth can be acquired at any moment. A poor individual might become rich overnight, while the wealthiest person could face sudden adversity and lose everything in mere seconds. However, those who lack loved ones around them always remain in a state of poverty. Love and relationships are not contingent on material possessions or fame. You, Avinash, are a genuinely good person with a pure heart—never let that change. Now, I should take my leave," she said, turning to depart.

Every word she said touched my heart. I felt like calling out to her and stopping her but my courage did not favour me.

Suddenly, she stopped, turned and said, I see a good friend in you. Let me know if you feel the same way. Take your time—there's no rush. She left smiling, and I kept looking at her.

I will be honoured to be your friend, Aditi, I said to myself.

A grand salutary ceremony waited for me at the hostel and began the moment I reached it. There was no more prolonged anger about what I did on the stage but some were very jealous of me for talking to Aditi that evening. Many people were teasing me. I was happy, smiling and feeling good, and I must admit that I was attracted to her.

"Will my brother be able to sleep today?" Suresh asked me teasingly.

"Shut up! Let me sleep. Tomorrow, there's an early-morning class," I replied blushingly.

I fell asleep thinking about her simplicity and thoughts.

The studies commenced with full intensity, and my father advised me to focus on my academic performance. Consequently, I did not even go home and dedicate myself to my studies. Aditi and I would often cross paths but our interactions were limited to mere greetings. Neither of us said anything beyond that. As the semester concluded, I managed to pass with excellent marks, while Aditi secured the top position in the batch. I contemplated expressing my pride and admiration for her achievement but I refrained from doing so.

It was a week's winter break. I was going home. I tried meeting Aditi before leaving but she was not at the university. I was a little upset but that was okay.

In the evening, I left and was waiting for a taxi at the university gate when a black Mercedes pulled up next to me. The window glass rolled down— it was her! Yes, *Aditi*!

"Quickly come, sit inside, Avinash, or else you will miss the train," she instructed.

She asked the driver to keep my bag in the car, and we left for the station.

"Congratulations!" I said.

"What for?" she asked, giving me a strange look.

"For being the topper," I replied.

"Oh, that way—it's not a big deal. Are you feeling bad that you came second?" she asked laughing teasingly.

"Weren't you on the university campus during the day?" I asked, pausing.

"Were you looking for me?" she asked, looking at me. She looked straight into my eyes.

Ignoring what she said, I replied, "Nice car! I am sitting in such a big car for the first time."

She looked at me for a while, smiled and said nothing.

She picked up a packet from the front seat and handed it to me. "This is for the little angels and your sister-in-law. Although I have never met her, I am sure she is very brave and courageous. May God bless her will strength and happiness," Aditi wished.

"Her name is Sonali," I said.

"And what was your brother's name?" she asked.

I replied, "Prakash."

"What happened to your brother?" she asked.

"He was murdered—shot dead," I replied.

She did not say anything but there was a feeling of care and concern in her eyes. We reached the station. She took a deep breath and said, "Okay, here we go. Happy journey! Stay safe!"

We shook hands—that was our first handshake. She smiled and said, "See you soon at the university. Have a good time."

I came back to Varanasi after a good time. My heart started to panic as soon as I stepped into the city. I reached home, and my father and Sonali were very happy to see me. Both the kids were angels—so cute, good-looking and twin bundles of joy!

I did not know why there was still pain and fear behind the smiles of Sonali and my father. They were hiding something from me. I asked them many times but my father avoided talking with me, and Sonali asked me to focus on my studies and career.

One day, when I went to the market, I met my friend, Manish. He was surprised and upset to see me. "What are you doing here?" he asked nervously.

"What do you mean? What kind of question is this? I have come to my home on vacation. Why are you asking me questions like this?" I asked.

"That means your father didn't tell you anything," he exclaimed.

"What's the matter? Will you say something or not?" I retorted.

"Bhairav and Rizvi are still causing trouble for your family," Manish conveyed with concern. "Rizvi constantly harasses Sonali in court by filing false cases against her, thus subjecting her to legal harassment. He even had the audacity to visit the hospital when she was giving birth to the kids. Rizvi persistently pressures Sonali to marry him, and he even threatened to take the kids under his control by turning them into slaves as they grow up. When your father objected, he faced severe physical assault, thus leaving him bedridden for days."

Manish continued, "Bhairav also creates chaos at your house, and he has used derogatory terms for Prakash's kids. Furthermore, he has threatened to harm you as well. This is why I was scared for your safety when I saw you here. Avinash, I beg you to leave this place and stay away from here," Manish pleaded with deep concern and urgency. "I might also get into trouble if anyone sees me with you," Manish added.

I came home very angry, upset and disappointed. I asked my father, "Why didn't you call me that evening? Why did Sonali talk to me from your phone?"

He replied without looking at me, "It was much-awaited good news for you and all of us. I thought it would be better if Sonali gave it to you personally."

"No, it's a lie," I retorted. "You both hide things from me. You guys are facing so much trouble—yet you won't tell me anything because you feel that I am weak—but it's not that. I know Bhairav and Rizvi are troubling you even today. And I will do what I must do. Enough is enough—no more."

"What will you do?" Sonali asked, her anger evident, a tone I had never experienced from her before.

"Yes, we both are facing immense troubles, and they are torturing us relentlessly. Now that you know about it, are you satisfied? It's alright. Please stay away from all this. Dad and I will handle it. You don't need to worry about us. Just focus on your career and avoid getting entangled in the affairs of Varanasi—there's nothing here for you. Your studies are almost complete. Excel in them, find a good job and settle down in a better place. That's what you wanted too, right? You made the same promise to Prakash, didn't you?" Sonali explained, laying out her thoughts to Avinash.

"Please, Avinash, don't involve yourself in this mess. Now, both of us are afraid of losing you. You are our last pillar of support and hope in life. Dad didn't keep anything from you, and we don't want to distract you from your goals. No matter how powerful evil may seem, it will ultimately crumble. Both Bhairav and Rizvi will face the consequences for every atrocity they've committed against us. We are fighting our legal battle, and I am certain that we will emerge victorious," she concluded, hoping to dissuade Avinash from intervening in their ongoing struggle.

It was already night-time, and the entire house was enveloped in silence. Sonali quietly entered my room and gently placed her hand on my head. "I'm sorry, you are my brother too, aren't you? Please don't be angry with me. I hope you can understand my concern and worry for you.

It's true that both Dad and I are often stressed, scared and feel helpless but nothing is as important to us as your life and your success. Dad may not say it but he has become very weak due to the situation. Anyways, cheer up now. Come to Dad's room, and let's have dinner together," Sonali said with genuine affection before leaving my room.

In the solitude of my room, I wept softly for some time. *Oh, Prakash, why did you have to leave us? You were the pillar of strength for Dad, Sonali and me. You had shown us how to live life with dignity and honour,* I thought.

It was almost midnight. Dad was awake, sitting on his chair, and Sonali, too, was working. "Is it not too late for you to go to sleep?" I asked her.

"Yes, I have a case tomorrow—I'm preparing for the same," she replied.

"Did you have dinner?" I asked. She looked at me, and said, "Do you think we can have our meals without you?"

I served Sonali and Dad some food, and we all ate together—after a long time.

The following day, I was ready to pack my bags.

"Where are you going?" Dad asked.

"Going back to Mumbai," I replied to him.

"There are still two more days left, isn't it? So why are you leaving early?" Dad asked.

"Just leaving, and now I will come back only when I solve your problems and can give you a better life. And you must listen to one thing—I am your son and Sonali's brother. I am both of your shadows. I will never leave you and am with you in every moment of happiness and sorrow."

I touched Father's and Sonali's feet and left.

Before heading back to Mumbai, there was one thing I needed to do. I left my belongings at Manish's house and made my way to Bhairav's office, where Rizvi was also present.

I was filled with fear—my feet trembled with every step. However, I recalled Prakash's words— "As long as we let fear control us, others will use it to intimidate us. If you remain afraid, others will continue to frighten you. But the one who conquers fear and faces it head-on ultimately emerges victorious."

Both were surprised to see me. I straightaway entered his office and sat in the chair opposite him.

"How dare you come here?" Bhairav asked threateningly.

"Stop troubling Dad and Sonali," I said in a firm voice.

Bhairav laughed out loudly for a long time and said, "Oh well, so you have come here to beg. Did your old father send you?"

Rizvi kept staring at me.

"I have not come here to beg, nor has my father sent me. I just came to see how cheap a brother can be. You didn't spare your sister from fulfilling that man's dirty ambition. He still bothers her despite her having two small kids to look after!"

"To hell with the kids! They are sinful, dirty-blooded, illegitimate, drain worms and they will be crushed!"

"You should not have dared to come here," Bhairav said and he ordered his goons and said, "Throw him out of here!"

"Be careful if anyone even touches me," I said, warning them. I do not know from where but somehow, I gathered a lot of courage.

"You both have done whatever you wanted to do. Now, I implore you—to leave me and my family alone. Take this as a request or a warning. We have endured enough because of you and it must all stop. I know you may perceive our pleas as a sign of weakness, thinking you can crush us like ants whenever you wish. But remember, even an ant can defeat an elephant. Put an end to all of this. We've had enough of you, and I sincerely hope we never have to cross paths with you and your family again!" I sternly declared before getting up to leave.

Suddenly, I felt a severe blow from behind, and it was Rizvi. I fell to the ground, face down, and he began to choke me with his leg.

"You are not mere ants. You are worms in a filthy drain! The same goes for your brother, his children and your father," Rizvi spat out with intense rage while clenching his teeth.

Just then, my father arrived—Manish must have informed him. He approached Rizvi and desperately pleaded, "Please, I beg of you, spare my son. Please let him go," he said, his voice quivering with tears.

Dad continued to plead relentlessly but my attempts to free myself were in vain. I felt utterly helpless and weak. Witnessing my father's condition, as he begged for my life, left me feeling even more ashamed and broken. Rizvi pushed him away and dealt a harsh blow to my face with a vicious kick.

"Take him away, old man, before I kill him too. If I ever see him in this city again, his death is certain. You've already attended one son's funeral. Do you want to attend another for your other son?" Rizvi warned my father menacingly.

Dad apologized to Rizvi and hurriedly led me away to a nearby Lord Shiva temple. Was it his love or concern for me? He kept slapping my face while crying bitterly. That day, I realized how deeply he loved me.

"I told you to stay away from all this! But you disobeyed! Leave us in this miserable condition and go away forever!" he demanded, his voice filled with pain and frustration.

My father placed my hand on his head and pleaded, "Swear on me and Lord Shiva that you will never come back here, no matter what."

With determination, I responded, "I don't need to swear by Lord Shiva. Swearing by your name is enough. I am going, and I will return only when you ask me to."

Feeling embarrassed, scared and broken, I left that place, gathering whatever little strength remained in me. I wanted to touch my father's feet as a sign of respect but he refused to allow me to do so.

That day, I learned a valuable lesson—that courage alone is not sufficient. One also needs immense strength. Lord Hanuman turned Ravana's Lanka into ashes single-handedly because he possessed both courage and strength. Additionally, it is crucial to assess the power of one's enemies. My foolish actions had led to this terrible suffering for my father today.

I returned to Mumbai, and for nearly 10 days, I secluded myself inside my hostel room. My face bore the scars of the injury, my spirit felt wounded and shame weighed heavily in my heart. I felt utterly helpless, and each passing day was filled with tears as I sought comfort in the embrace of my friend, Suresh. He took exceptional care of me, offering consolation and solace during those trying times.

One day, to my surprise, Aditi came looking for me at the hostel. Suresh had informed her about everything that had happened. It was evening, and I sat alone in the dimly lit room.

"Why is there so much darkness here? Doesn't your room have proper lighting, or has the hostel administration not paid the electricity bill?" Aditi questioned as she swiftly turned on the lights.

With a smile, she commented, "Although the room seems decent, the interiors need some work, or else I won't come again."

Her presence there was unexpected. After all, it was a men's hostel, and I couldn't comprehend why she would come for me. As she gazed at me, her eyes filled with tears.

"Would you like to have some tea, Avinash?" she asked, her smile shining through the concern.

I nodded, replying, "Yes, please."

Aditi asked Suresh to bring tea and then approached me closely. She began applying medicine to my facial wounds. "Light is needed to dispel darkness," she uttered thoughtfully.

Extending her hand towards me, she said, "Avinash, let's conquer this darkness and move towards a brighter future of hope and prosperity, leaving this pain behind. As your friend, I promise that I will never let you be enveloped in darkness again."

I embraced her tightly, and tears started flowing uncontrollably. "Save me, Aditi. I feel suffocated in this darkness. I don't want to die. I want to live and achieve something in life. I wish to be someone, to do something that will make everyone proud someday."

She consoled me with tender understanding—treating me with utmost care, just like a small child in need of comfort. She kept comforting and empathizing with me— showing genuine concern and support.

"Ahm…Ahm…Tea is here, my friends," Suresh said while forwarding cups towards Aditi and me.

That evening was a breath of fresh air after such a long and difficult time. We laughed, cheered, shared stories, danced and, of course, endured Suresh's endless collection of pathetic jokes. I named that day *Friendship Day*, as it marked the strengthening of our bond and togetherness. Soon, my room was filled with men and women—some were my hostel mates, while others were Aditi's friends. Together, we decided to visit Marine Drive, one of the most beautiful spots in Mumbai. I had often observed people sitting there quietly, lost in their thoughts, having heartfelt conversations with the sea, expressing joy or releasing their frustrations and pain. There was something unique about this place—it had a way of making you feel at ease.

As we all sat facing the sea, we spent hours simply watching the waves. The time had flown by, and it was midnight. The cold breeze that passed through our ears sent shivers down our spines but it was strangely comforting. We were all in a state of calm, and everyone wore smiles on their faces. Yet everyone's eyes had been brimming with tears. It felt like we all shared a part of our pain and emotions with the ocean as if it understood and empathized with our struggles.

"Do you see these waves, Avinash?" Aditi asked.

"The sea is vast and possesses immense power, speed and force. Its waves move forward but also get pulled back. Do you know what's truly essential? It's how far they move ahead each time. Life, too, resembles these waves. As we progress forward, we may encounter setbacks but the key is to keep moving ahead and rising higher with every challenge we face—that's what truly matters. What happened to you and your family was beyond your control. However, what you can do now is within your grasp. You have the power to take charge and steer your life in a positive direction, creating value in everything that comes your way," Aditi suggested.

"I understand that it's not easy, and it won't be, considering all that you have endured and continue to face. No one else can fully comprehend your pain, suffering and suffocation—only you can truly feel that. But remember, it's up to you to decide how long you remain entangled in your problems," she added with empathy and wisdom.

"I am trying, Aditi," I said.

"Trying?" she asked and laughed.

"There's no such thing as *trying* in this world. We either do it or we don't. Don't use *trying* or *tried but could not do* as shields to justify failure or gain sympathy from others," Aditi firmly expressed her perspective.

I nodded in agreement, looking at her with newfound admiration. Time had flown by, and before we knew it, the sunrise was approaching. Aditi and I had not slept the whole night, while our other friends were peacefully asleep, resting on the cold sand or leaning against stones and the ground.

As the sun rose, Aditi and I walked to the sea. Playing with the waves, I felt a release as I shed my pains, fears and worries into the vast ocean. My vision, once blurred, now seemed clearer. I made a silent vow to myself that I would accomplish something meaningful in my life to make my father proud once again. I pledged to stand strong and unwavering beside my family and loved ones, determined and unstoppable. That sunrise marked the beginning of a new chapter in my life.

Eventually, everyone woke up, and we all enjoyed coffee and Mumbai's famous *Vadapav* together. As we headed back to the hostel, we dropped Aditi off at her grand bungalow—a sight that did not surprise me, since I knew about her affluent background. However, my other friends—especially Suresh, were fascinated by her luxurious home. Our perception of her had changed. We had previously thought of her as a high-headed and arrogant person, given her social status but she turned out to be humble, sensible and mature. All of us had become friends, and we were genuinely delighted with that newfound bond.

Some people thought that Aditi was falling in love with me—what a humorous thought that was! She had entered my life as a great friend and a pillar of support, and I felt incredibly happy and blessed.

Life was gradually falling back into place. I immersed myself in my studies, and an excellent internship opportunity came my way at a leading FMCG company, which was crucial for my course. I was overjoyed with the opportunity.

Sonali frequently called to inquire about my well-being and shared news about her children, Prakash and Pallavi. She repeatedly invited me to visit home but I kept declining. Deep down, I wanted to go—but something held me back.

Time flew by, and before I knew it, the final semester of my course had arrived, and campus placements were underway. I secured a position in a renowned multinational company in the telecom industry. It was an incredible feeling, and I immediately called Dad to share the news. Though he did not say much, I could sense his happiness.

Suresh also landed a great job in a big IT company, and our other friends found good placements too. Aditi chose to join her mother's fashion business.

On 11th March—Aditi's birthday, she invited us to a party at her home. She expressed that we were all about to embark on a new chapter in our lives in different places and cities, which was why she wanted to celebrate her birthday with all her friends. Her words stirred something within me, and I could not shake off the fear of losing her and going away. Was I falling in love with her?

We arrived at her venue for the grand celebration, which was reminiscent of scenes from movies where a poor boy attends the birthday party of a girl from an affluent family. Many guests, including Aditi's friends, were present. Suresh and I seemed like the most ordinary-looking ones amongst the guests. She was delighted to see all of us.

Aditi looked stunning, and it was hard to take my eyes off her. I offered her a bouquet and she introduced me to her other friends and a few relatives. Curiously, I asked about her parents, but she seemed to brush off the question and shifted the topic. She kindly offered me a cold drink using the waiter's assistance but her reaction to my question made me wonder if it had upset her. She soon got busy greeting others, and it was time for her to cut the birthday cake.

"I will do whatever I wish to—you shouldn't dare to ask anything of me, you bitch!"

A loud voice caught everyone's attention. It was Aditi's father, highly drunk, holding the hand of a young woman.

Aditi's mother was following them both, and trying to stop him. "At least, not today," she requested him. "It's her birthday! Don't make her feel embarrassed," pleaded Aditi's mother.

"This is my house! You need not tell me when and how I need to come home. Oh, yes, it's my lovely daughter's birthday, so let's celebrate," said Aditi's father.

He held Aditi's hand and forcefully made her cut the cake, thus spoiling it. He took some cake in his hand and rubbed it all over Aditi's mother's face. Saying "Best wishes on your daughter's birthday, you ugly bitch," he left with the younger woman.

Aditi stood with her eyes downcast—appearing scared and embarrassed. Her mother kept crying and hid her face while standing in a corner of their garden. All the guests started leaving. Aditi's mother apologized to everyone with folded hands and went inside the house.

Suresh asked me to go, but I did not move. Today my friend needed me—how could I leave her alone?

"Please have some water," I said, offering a glass of water to her.

I cleaned the cake from her hands with a tissue.

"You should go from here, Avinash, leave me alone with my shame, please," she said without looking at me.

"Look at me, Aditi. Please don't do this to yourself. You have not done anything wrong. Please calm down," I said while requesting her to sit.

She sat down. Tears began to flow from her eyes.

"I knew it—knew it very well! Why did I arrange this party? Don't I know my father well enough? Foolish me, I wanted to celebrate my birthday with my friends and at my house. In this big house, that's what you all say, right? I live in this vast house and have no right or freedom to do things as per *my* wish. Do you know, Avinash? I knew that my father could create a ruckus anytime. Mother said '*no*' and suggested hosting this party somewhere outside. Ahh, stupid me, I didn't listen to her. Because of my father's pride and his wrong attitude, no one wanted to come to our house except his so-called high society's fake people.

He does not consider anyone as anything more important than his money and status. Do you know who that woman was—the one who was with my father? She was my friend—my father made her my friend from the high society, who today, wants to take my mother's place in our house! I was never given the freedom to make friends. My friends were always judged by their status and that of their family members. I was forced only to be friends with people who belonged in his high society friends' families. I was so happy to be associated with you, Suresh and my other college friends. I wanted to cherish, celebrate and remember this all my life. I never thought that this party would turn out to be so ugly like this. I am alone again—desperate and helpless," Aditi kept saying while she stood crying.

Upset with herself, and in so much pain, Aditi was scared of losing all her friends—and me. She was scared that we might all stop talking to her. Who could have thought a woman from such a renowned family, who had wealth, fame and status had so much loneliness?

"Why have you never spoken to me, Aditi? I am your friend. I could have helped you understand and taken care of you," I said, gently holding her hand.

"Do you know, Avinash, when our sorrows become overwhelming? It's when the whole world becomes aware of them. Regardless of whether we are rich, poor, young, or old, we all experience pain, face disappointments and confront fears. Each one of us carries our battles and worries. What we present to the world is often not reflective of what lies within. We walk around wearing masks—projecting a facade of happiness. We care for ourselves daily, trying hard to convince ourselves that everything is fine or will eventually be fine. People gauge our emotions based on the brightness of the masks we wear, assuming whether we are happy or sad. But how much can one truly judge just by appearance or social status? Who takes the time to explore our hearts? Sadly, no one."

"If only someone would look deeper, they would find a profound need for that one person who can unconditionally support, comfort and hold us close. Nothing in the world, no wealth, stature or material possession can compare to the value of that special individual. The problem, however, is that while we all desire to find that person, we often forget to be that person for someone else."

"Many people may claim to want to be with me, but are they genuine? The answer, more often than not, is *no*. They are attracted by my family's status, not by who I truly am. But do you know what, Avinash? We can always identify that one right and genuine person amidst the crowd. However, it doesn't happen easily—that's why I didn't confide in you earlier. There have been numerous times when I felt like crying on your shoulder, but I hesitated. I wasn't sure how you would perceive me or what you would understand. I've always tried not to cry, even in solitude, as I don't believe that it's productive. I also fear that someone might catch me crying and show me unnecessary sympathy."

"Today, everything just became overwhelming, and my tears couldn't be contained any longer. I feel embarrassed that it happened in front of everyone, but I couldn't help it," Aditi confessed, her voice laden with emotion.

"I'm glad that at least you asked me—why didn't you share any of this?" I asked her.

"You see, this is what I am. I have everything but own nothing. I am very rich but equally poor. I am weak and broken. So, tell me, do you still want to be my friend? Come on, tell me…" she said, emphasizing her feelings.

Her eyes were glistening with moisture as they stared at me. I had an overwhelming urge to hold her tightly in my arms—to comfort her like one would soothe a small child, and assure her that I would be there for her today, tomorrow and always. I could not help but be drawn to her brilliance, brightness and intelligence. With just one look from her, my mind would ease, and my heart would be filled with joy. Her presence seemed to dispel the darkness around me, making me feel safe and at peace.

Her social status and wealth were never the reasons for initiating our friendship. I admired her not because she was weak but because she displayed courage and strength that was far greater than mine. Despite her struggles and feelings of loneliness, she still extended her helping hand to support me.

Lost in my thoughts, I had not realized that she was still gazing at me, and perhaps awaiting my response. Before I could say anything, she spoke gently, "There's no rush, Avinash. Take your time and let me know when you are sure and confident. Friendship and relationships are lifelong commitments, and one should not decide hastily, by being driven by emotions or circumstances. True commitment comes with unwavering trust, and when the other person believes in our commitment, it becomes an integral part of their life. You know what? Trust is blind, and it has always been that way. If we don't wholeheartedly believe in something, it cannot be truly trusted," she expressed.

"Now go, Avinash. It's already too late," she added.

Oh, what did she just say? The expression in her eyes spoke louder than her words. I had already surrendered myself to her. Yes, I was madly in love with her. As I walked away from her home, every part of me felt like it was left behind—with her. I wanted to tell her, *Please take care* but she kept looking away, towards another direction. I turned back several times, hoping she would glance at me—but she did not. Perhaps she expected too much from me. Maybe there were many things that she wanted to say but she held them back. Her silence seemed to carry a mixture of anger, sadness and a desire for solitude.

Loneliness engulfed her, and she appeared to want to be alone in that moment. Her mother kept watching us from a window for a long time. I left Aditi sitting there, in the stillness of the night. Every part of me wanted her to stop me—for her to call out, "Don't go, Avinash!" But it did not happen.

I continued walking, desperately hoping to hear her voice urging me to stay. But the words I yearned for never came.

After that day, Aditi and I did not cross paths intentionally. Even though she continued coming to college, she deliberately avoided meeting or speaking with me. It was as if I had become invisible to her. The day had finally arrived when we were all ready to bid farewell to our college lives and embark on our respective professional journeys. It was our final day at college—the Farewell

Day—and we were filled with mixed feelings of happiness, excitement and energy. After all, we had all secured fantastic placements—particularly those who were in our close-knit friend group.

Our dean addressed the students with the following words: "Dear students, as you move away from your support system, namely your parents and teachers, it is time to embrace maturity and make sensible decisions. Forge meaningful connections and relationships by earning trust. Remember to not just rely on your logical mind but also to listen to your heart. Otherwise, you might find yourself alone one day. When you feel stuck, let your heart guide you and trust your instincts."

"While it is important to strive for financial success and social standing, it should not come at the expense of compromising your values, relationships or dignity. Whether it is dealing with clients, business associates, colleagues, relatives, friends, life partners or anyone else, maintaining trust and belief in others is crucial and should be unconditional."

"In this world, trust and belief are powerful forces that often operate beyond rationality—and they should. Just as we have not seen God, we can still feel the influence of an unseen, divine power, and it is this same trust that we bestow upon it."

"My dear young men and women, I urge you to preserve your humanity and not become mere machines. Spread love, happiness and care to everyone around you. Focus on making a name for yourself through your actions, and money and stature will naturally follow. While you dedicate yourself to helping others, don't forget to cherish and value that one person in your life whom you trust implicitly or who trusts you blindly. Such a relationship is a priceless asset that will enrich your life profoundly."

"These are some of the important lessons that I wanted to share with you on your last day at this university. I sincerely wish you all great success and growth in your lives!"

Our dean had left and what remained was deep silence in the hall. A few students stood with moist eyes and a few waited with a smile. They all looked at each other. A few hugged their friends, and many cried.

Is that *one person*, *trust* and *belief* so important? Indeed, Prakash was the one for Dad, me, and Sonali till now, who gave us so much strength.

I looked at Aditi. She was smiling and talking to her friends. We looked at each other after a long time, or to be precise, after 97 days. I waved to her from quite a distance. She responded with her beautiful smile. However, it seemed like she was ignoring me. The loud noise of the DJ electrified everyone's minds. We started celebrating the beginning of our new lives by dancing and cheering. There was a lot of noise around us, as well as joyful and smiling faces. I was smiling too, and a little high but something was bothering me. It seemed as though I was leaving behind something essential.

I wanted to speak to Aditi. I had to ask her something and reply to what she asked me the other day. Although I was a little drunk but still in control, I approached her.

"I have two job offers, one in Bangalore and the other in Mumbai. Which one should I choose?" I asked her.

She looked at me for a while and said, "Are you choosing cities or opportunities?"

I replied abruptly, "You will not be in Bangalore!"

Looking surprised, she crinkled her brows and replied, "Can we move out from here? It's too noisy."

She asked her driver to go home. "How will you go then?" I asked.

"Maybe you can drop me today," she said, looking deeply into my eyes.

We kept walking for a while, but we did not say anything.

It was evening. The weather was bad, and a strong wind blew. Maybe it was going to rain.

"Have you drunk for the first time today?" she asked.

I replied hesitantly, "No…I did…once or twice in the hostel when it was someone's birthday."

"You didn't answer my question, Aditi," I reminded her.

"Why are you doing this, Avinash? Don't do this, please! Am I so important that you are still indecisive about your job acceptance? It's a beginning you were looking forward to—to support your family. Choose an opportunity that helps you scale up high and most importantly, makes you happy and meets your career aspiration. You can't be emotional about this—think sensibly and logically. I will always want you to grow and do your best in your life—from wherein all this has come, I don't understand…Choose what is best! After all, we are friends, right? We can meet anytime," she replied in a heavy voice.

Her eyes were moist. "Please go, do good in life, and trust me, I will be the happiest person for you always!"

Amidst the resounding thunderclaps and the brilliant flashes of lightning, a torrential downpour veiled her tears. However, her emotions remained unmistakably evident within the depths of her eyes. Was this a manifestation of her affection for me, or merely a poignant instance as she bid farewell to a friend, potentially for the last time on the closing day of college?

As for me, it marked the ache of parting from her—leaving behind not just a friend but the person I had fallen deeply in love with. I yearned to be by her side for the remainder of my days, and on this day, regardless of her response, I resolved to declare my love.

That was the moment for me and I decided to tell her how much I loved her. A man from Uttar Pradesh does not propose to a woman. Instead, he directly asks for her hand in marriage and I did so.

Forgetting that we were walking on the side of the road, I gently took her hand and said, "Aditi, you were right about trust—it's always blind, and if it isn't, it's not trust. You can trust me blindly. I will never betray you. My love for you will be everlasting. I promise to care for you, protect you and respect you always. Aditi, I love you. Will you marry me?"

Tenderly, I kissed her forehead.

Upon hearing my words, she gazed at me for a moment and then tightly embraced me while she sobbed uncontrollably. I held her—trying to console her like one would comfort a child. It was late in the evening and the weather was still tumultuous. Suddenly, a car horn sounded, and a police officer from the PCR vehicle spoke, "Are you kids indulging in romance on the road tonight? It's very late, and the weather is terrible too. Go home, you silly youngsters!"

Ignoring the inspector's interruption, I continued to hold Aditi close—reassuring her that everything would be alright. At that moment, I knew that no matter what challenges lay ahead, we would face them together, bound by the unbreakable trust and love that we shared for each other.

He went away after scolding us.

With laughter echoing in the air, we looked back at the inspector, feeling amused by his interruption, and then joyfully fled from the scene. When you are in love, the world transforms into a beautiful place, and every worry seems to vanish. Hand in hand, we dashed towards Juhu Beach with our hearts pounding with excitement.

As we reached the beach, the unspoken love between us hung in the air, waiting to find its voice. Aditi moved closer to me. Although my heart raced with nervousness and shyness, I could feel affectionate energy enveloping us. Finally, the moment arrived when our emotions overflowed, and we shared our first kiss—a tender expression of love amidst the first spell of rain.

The rain poured down heavily, and the sea waves surged around us, adding to the enchanting ambience. We embraced each other, our lips meeting again and again— both lost in the magic of the moment. Time seemed to stand still as we let our love speak through the sweet cadence of the rain and the passionate exchange of kisses. It felt like an eternity of blissful affection amidst the wild storm and the roaring waves.

Aditi said, "I love you, Avinash, and yes, I will marry you!"

The Love Song:

(Verse 1)

The rain is falling down,

As we stand here by the shore,

The waves crash at our feet,

But we don't mind anymore.

(Chorus)

I've loved you since the moment I met you,

And every day my love grows stronger,

Will you take my hand and be my forever,

As we stand here in the rain by the water.

(Verse 2)

I know we've had our ups and downs,

But through it all my love has stayed true,

I want to spend forever with you,

And make all your dreams come true.

(Chorus)

I've loved you since the moment I met you,

And every day, my love grows stronger,

Will you take my hand and be my forever,

As we stand here in the rain by the water.

(Bridge)

I promise to love you always,

To be there for you in every way,

Together we can conquer anything,

As we start this new chapter, with love and with a ring.

(Chorus)

I've loved you since the moment I met you,

And every day my love grows stronger,

Will you take my hand and be my forever,

As we stand here in the rain by the water.

(Outro)

So, let's take this step together,

And create a love that lasts forever,

As we stand here in the rain by the sea,

I promise to always love and cherish thee.

With no other wishes left unfulfilled, we were overflowing with happiness, joy and cheerfulness. We made a decision together—I would take up the job in Bangalore since it offered better pay and prospects, while Aditi planned to extend her mother's business in the same city. Despite the distance, we remained connected, and I frequently travelled back to Mumbai to be with her.

Aditi's mother was delighted with our relationship and supported us wholeheartedly. However, as we anticipated, Aditi's father strongly opposed our union. Nevertheless, we persevered, and after a year and a half, we decided to tie the knot. I informed Dad and Sonali. Although my dad did not speak to me directly, Sonali conveyed his happiness for me.

When I went to meet Aditi's parents, her father refused to see me and demanded that I leave their house immediately and urged me to stay away from Aditi's life. Despite the opposition, we got married in a modest ceremony with only a few guests who attended it. My father did not attend the wedding but did speak to Aditi via video call. Sonali, on the other hand, graced the occasion with her presence, and her children had grown up beautifully.

Aditi and I relocated to Bangalore, thus embarking on a new chapter in our lives. Throughout this journey, her mother stood by us and offered her unwavering support in every possible way. Though she never uttered a word of disapproval or asked any probing questions, her eyes often carried unspoken inquiries, which sought to understand our choices and decisions. Her silent gaze conveyed a mixture of concern, love and curiosity, and made us realize how much she cared for our happiness and well-being. Despite not voicing her thoughts, her presence and affectionate gestures spoke volumes, and we were grateful for her constant presence in our lives as we settled into our new home in Bangalore.

One day, while she was returning to Mumbai. We were on our way to the airport.

"Can I ask you something?" I spoke.

She looked at me, smiled and said, "You are like my son, and a son doesn't need permission from a mother. I know you have many questions, and I am here to reply."

"Why did you agree to our wedding and go against your husband and many other relatives? It was difficult for you to manage things while Aditi and I were getting married," I asked.

"Hmm…you have a few more things to ask, and let me guess. You feel you don't match up to our family's standards—that you're not rich like us, etc., isn't it?" she replied, looking at me.

"I saw the friend in you, the one who loves Aditi deeply and will take care of her for the rest of her life, and that's why I agreed to your relationship. On Aditi's birthday, when you came home and everything unfolded, I observed you very carefully. The way you cared for her, the affection you showed and how you comforted and pacified her—I noticed it all. Aditi is not one to openly express her feelings—she keeps everything hidden in her heart. She relies on you a great deal and loves you deeply, even though she might not say it out loud. I am certain that you will understand her without her having to say a word. She has complete faith in you, more than in anyone else in this world. She believes that you will be by her side forever, until her last breath. How could I say no to such trust, faith and love?"

"When you left that evening, I saw how you held yourself back and yearned to be with her but felt helpless. It was at that moment that I made the decision never to come between your love and to ensure that no one else would either. Any mother would want a man like you for her daughter. Avinash, money is nothing—it can be earned anytime, and so can status and fame. But finding a true life partner is not so easy. I have everything in terms of wealth and status but I could never find that one person who could truly understand, comfort and support me, especially during my lowest moments. I am delighted that Aditi found you, and I know she is in good hands. You are the person she needs in her life, and I wholeheartedly support your relationship," Aditi's mother expressed with warmth and sincerity.

"Very few people have the courage to fight with their past, struggle in the present and ride smoothly towards their future. You are that one, Avinash. Aditi is so proud of you—so, do I."

"Please take care of yourself because, only then, will Aditi be fine and happy. I know who you are for her."

We reached the airport, and I hugged her tightly, saying, "Thank you so much for giving Aditi to me."

She smiled and left for Mumbai.

That day, for the first time, I felt so much love for myself. I could not believe that I could give someone great happiness, make her smile and give her a life. I just wanted to reach home as early as possible—to my Aditi.

(Doorbell rang.)

She opened the door.

I reached home, knelt down and presented a big bouquet of red roses to her.

She said, smiling and holding the bouquet, "Have you come flying all the way?"

I lifted her in my arms and said, "I love you—I love you very much."

"Put me down, Avinash. Are you mad? People are watching," she said and laughed.

A voice reached us that said, "Oh, so sweet."

He was our neighbour, Jagdeep Singh. He left laughing.

I helped Aditi down, and she went inside the house shyly. The house was decorated with scented candles, and she had made delicious food.

I made her sit in front of me and fed her food with my hands. I said, "Why do you love me so much? Now tell me how to live without you."

She kissed my forehead and said, "Who told you to live without me? I am your shadow, Avinash. No one can separate you from me even after I die."

"Shut up. You are not going to die before me. If death is inevitable, I will go after you. You are my responsibility, and I will complete it."

I knew she never liked to listen to that *shut-up* phrase, but I had to tell her today.

Aditi had settled in my soul, my life—my everything.

It was the most beautiful night of my life and a new beginning for us. Life was amazing—there was a massive success in my career, lots of friends, college union parties and the most special part was Mr. and Mrs. Jagdeep Singh's elderly support. Soon, they became like family—not just our neighbours.

Much success was stored for Aditi and me, along with happiness and a wonderful life. I always dreamt of supporting Dad and Sonali. Yes, I could do it. Aditi and I often used to speak to Sonali but Dad used to talk to Aditi only, not me. Maybe he was still angry with me.

With the blessings of Lord Shiva, we joyously welcomed a baby boy into our lives, whom we named Aditya. He brought an indescribable sense of completeness and fulfilment. Every desire in our hearts had been granted, and we felt truly blessed.

On the day Aditya was born, I had a heartfelt video call with my father. He looked so happy, his eyes glistening with tears of joy. He said, "I miss you so much, my son. I am overjoyed that my brave little child has become a father today. Now that I have seen my grandson as well, I can peacefully depart from this world and climb the golden ladder to heaven. May God grant me that time."

It was a touching moment, and I could feel the love and happiness radiating through the screen. Aditya's arrival had brought immense joy not only to us but also to my father, who was sure that his lineage would continue and prosper. With the blessing of his grandson, he found a sense of fulfilment and contentment. We were grateful for the love and support from both our families, and Aditya's birth marked the beginning of a beautiful new chapter in our lives.

He laughed while kissing and showering his love and affection for Aditya.

"Can I come and see you, Dad?" I asked him.

I thought he would say *yes*, but he denied it. "Avinash, ask me anything but never should you come back here. I am so happy to see you growing and now I see my grandson. Just stay there," he spoke.

"Why don't you come here for a few days if I can't come?" I pleaded.

"I will come—I will come for sure," he said.

I still needed to be necessary there, and he disconnected the call. I do not know what he was still hiding from me. There was something that his eyes were saying but not the words.

Life there was beautiful—smiling at us. Aditi's immense love and Aditya's presence filled my life with bliss. It was fun, peaceful and excellent. Leaving all my sorrows behind, I realized that I had come a long way.

Our bundle of joy, Aditya grew up in no time. I was less his father and more his friend.

To play, hang out and have fun—that was how we interacted. I started reliving my childhood. He wanted to do things that I could not do with his mother. Five years had passed.

One day, I was taking a bath, and Aditi knocked on the door.

"Avinash, how much time do you need? Mom has called many times. She wants to speak to you."

I came out and saw Aditi taking our luggage bags.

"Are we going somewhere?" I asked.

Before she could reply, my phone rang—it was my mother-in-law.

"Hello, Avinash, how are you doing, my son?" she asked.

Greeting her, I replied, "I am doing good."

Hesitatingly she asked, "Aditya's birthday is next week. Is it possible for you all to celebrate it here in Mumbai? He has never been here. I am sure he would love coming here and even meeting us as well," she requested.

Us? Would it be acceptable for him to come to *that* house? In all these years, my father-in-law never even talked to Aditi and me. Aditya was five years old. He never asked for Aditya too.

"Do you think we should come? I mean, to your home?" I asked.

"Don't worry, plenty of time has passed. I am sure that after seeing Aditya, his heart will melt, and his anger will subside. He will hug Aditya. I know he has not treated you right. But now both of us are getting old and I wish that our grandson would come to our house—at least once. And what could be the best occasion but this fifth birthday?" she requested.

I could see everything in life but not Aditi's tears. Even without saying anything, her eyes said everything.

I hugged her and said, "I don't want your father to insult you again. Nor do I want to create any lousy memory for Aditya of his grandfather. I cannot stop you from meeting your father. If you are sure, let's go."

She hugged me and smiled.

Aditya was always fond of travelling, and he was excited about Mumbai. His list was prepared and it was quite impressive. He explored the internet well and found information about the city of Mumbai. His utmost priority was to visit the science museum, the Elephanta cave, the Gateway of India and boating.

A day before our departure, Aditi's father texted her:

The doors of my house were closed for you yesterday, today and forever. Yes, if you leave that two-penny man and come, you can come. Seeing the face of that poor man makes me suffocate. I will get you married according to our status. Until then, forget about my house and don't even dare to enter Mumbai. Otherwise, I will throw your mother out along with you.

Hate and relationships have an intense connection. If a person is determined, he is prepared to sacrifice his relations in the fire of hatred.

Aditi was fuming with anger. Her self-respect and esteem were severely hurt. She never wanted her mother to suffer and did not want to break Aditya's heart as he was so excited to go to Mumbai. We decided to go to Mumbai, stay at Hotel Taj and celebrate his birthday there.

It is often said that if difficulties arise in any task, it may be a sign that it should not be pursued. This adage seemed to ring true in both Aditi's father's disapproval of our relationship and the challenges at my office. Despite the obstacles, we carried on—navigating through life's ups and downs.

On a particular day, I had to stay back at my office due to a crucial delegation visit. Thus, I dropped Aditi and Aditya off at the airport, and they flew to Mumbai. The following day, it was my turn to join them. Aditi's mother had also joined them, and Aditya was overjoyed to have everyone together. He embarked on a city tour, excitedly showing me the views of Mumbai via video call while eagerly anticipating my arrival.

Aditya's birthday was on November 26, a day I had always looked forward to since his birth. Our lives revolved around our child, and I continued to prioritize Aditya's happiness above all else. His smile had the power to erase any weariness that I felt on tough days. The touch of his little hands rejuvenated my spirit, and his innocent questions never failed to bring a smile to my face. His presence in our lives was a constant reminder of the immense joy and love that parenthood brought us.

My flight to Mumbai was delayed. I boarded around 5:00 p.m. and was scheduled to reach around 7:00 p.m. Aditya kept calling me throughout the whole day and was angry about my late arrival. Aditi and her mom made a fantastic arrangement for his birthday, and I was only waiting.

Mumbai, 7:30 p.m.: I left the airport for Hotel Taj Mahal Palace.

Aditi called, and asked, "Where have you reached? How much time will you take?"

"Ideally, 21 minutes…the rest depends on traffic…it's a working day," I replied.

"Okay, please speak to him—he is so impatient now," Aditi said, handing over the phone to Aditya.

"Hey, champ! What's up, my birthday boy? What's your party plan?" I asked.

"Dad, this is not done. Why are you so late?" he said and expressed that he was upset.

"Oh, don't be upset, my love, just 30 minutes to go and I will be there for your grand birthday celebration!" I said excitedly.

"Yippie!" he said and smiled with joy.

"Dad, this is such a fantastic place. I am in love with this place. Mom and Grandmother got beautiful decorations and a Pokémon cake!" he said, giggling.

"Let me show you. Can you make a video call on Mom's phone, please?" he spoke.

I replied with a *yes* and made a video call to speak with him.

Delighted with happiness, he ran around the hotel. First, he showed me the restaurant where his birthday decorations were being made, second, the sea view from the lobby and third, the Gateway of India.

"Dad, there are many people with golden hair too."

I laughed out loud and replied, "They are foreigners."

"Foreigners?" he asked.

"Yes, people from other countries visiting us," I replied.

"But why have they come here?" he asked anxiously.

"They have come for a holiday or work, my son," I said.

"Okay, just like we have come here, right?" he asked.

"Exactly!" I spoke.

He was out of breath while he continued running but he was having fun.

"Aditya, be careful and be with Mom only. You might fall and get hurt," I warned.

"Yes, I'm careful, don't worry. How long will it take to reach?" he asked.

I replied, "Finding some traffic…reaching at the earliest moment. Now you go back to Mom and sit with her."

He started going towards Aditi. "Wait while I go to Mummy," he spoke.

Aditi was reading a book and was sitting by the pool. Aditya was about to reach her when…

A tragic turn of events occurred when a bullet struck Aditi in the head. Aditya felt terrified and his mind was filled with fear. He rushed to her side but to his dismay, she was already gone. He began crying inconsolably, his young voice filled with anguish and confusion.

"Dad, look what happened to Mom! She's bleeding! She's lying there, and she's not responding!" he sobbed, desperately seeking comfort and understanding in the face of this devastating loss.

"Aditya, what happened there? Don't stop the video call. Where is your grandmother?" I asked nervously.

There was chaos in the hotel. People were seen and heard running, crying and shouting. It seemed as if someone was firing indiscriminately.

"Brother, please drive fast. My son's life is in danger."

Feeling nervous and pleading, I told the taxi driver to take me to the hotel.

There was much traffic, which kept increasing as I approached the hotel. Something had happened in the city. The police were putting up barricades. People were running on the streets.

"Please drive faster," I said, crying.

"What should I do, Sir? The car is not moving at all. The whole road is choked."

Aditya was very scared and was crying loudly. "Aditya, where is your grandmother? Run for your life and go to her."

"Dad, Mother is alone here. She is asleep. She is bleeding from her head and not even getting up. Many people, do not know why they are firing. How can I leave my mother alone?" he said, sobbing.

"Listen, Aditya, your mother will be fine. I will take care of her. Please save your life and run away to your grandmother," I instructed.

"Grandmother must be in the room. She was sleeping," he replied.

"Do you know the way?" I asked.

"Yes," he replied.

"Please run," I said.

I ran too and was moving out of the taxi. I was running madly on the road, and Aditya was in the hotel. People ran wherever the phone's camera went. Bodies were lying on the ground. There was fire and smoke. Several masked men were firing bullets.

I was screaming instructions to Aditya, and said, "Run my child, run! Save your life, and hide somewhere!"

He kept running.

Calling me, he said, "Father, save me."

He kept running and calling out to me, saying "Father, save me. Save me, please."

He either collided with something or was hit, and he fell.

"Dad, where are you? When will you come? It's hurting a lot. I can't see you. Where are you?" he cried loudly.

The phone's screen was broken, but the call was still on. I could see him, but he couldn't.

"To whom is he talking? Is he recording something? Check the phone," said a voice that approached my ears.

There was somebody around him. The phone was lying somewhere. I could only hear their voices but I could not see them. Aditya was moaning in pain.

"Are you hurt, Aditya?" I shouted.

"Shh...I hear someone's voice," the man said, sensing a presence on the phone call.

"The phone was picked up by one of the men—he was a terrorist. Is there someone on the call?" he asked, with suspicion evident in his tone.

"Please, I beg you, leave my son alone. He's just a small child. Spare him, please," I pleaded, my voice trembling with fear.

I could see his face clearly, but he remained unaware of my identity.

"Who are you?" he demanded, his voice filled with menace.

"I am Avinash. He is my son. Please, I implore you, don't hurt him. He's just a child. Please, have mercy and help him—save him," I pleaded, hoping my words would touch his heart.

"Save him?" he scoffed, letting out a menacing laugh. "We are here to kill, not to save. Nobody will be spared," he declared coldly, leaving me with a sinking feeling of despair.

The gravity of the situation weighed heavily upon me, as I desperately tried to protect my innocent son from this impending danger.

"Please, please, please, no, don't…please," I continuously requested him.

He could not see me but I was on my knees, begging him to spare Aditya's life with folded hands.

"Let him go, Murtaza. He is a small child. Poor boy will die on his own," someone said. It was probably another terrorist.

"No, no, no, Gafoor, brother had said, *no mercy.* Everyone must be killed, be it a child, someone old or young."

"Do you want to say something to your father before you die?" Murtaza asked in a teasing voice.

There was a sound of gunfire. He turned the phone towards Aditya and said, "I don't know if you can see your son or not. I killed him, and whoever obstructs the work of Allah will have the same fate. Whomever it is."

Aditya was covered in blood—he had shot Aditya. He breathed his last in front of my eyes and said, *"Miss You, Dad."*

My throat went dry, and I could neither cry nor let my voice come out. Gafoor was laughing out loud and probably threw the phone on the floor. The call was disconnected.

I rushed to the hotel, my mind consumed with despair and my eyes streaming with tears. Fear gripped my trembling body, and I felt as if my world was collapsing around me. The unimaginable had happened—my beloved wife and my child were brutally taken from me, right before my eyes. The sight was too much to bear, and I felt like I was losing my sanity.

As I approached the hotel, police barricades surrounded it from all sides. I pleaded and begged them to let me go inside and to check on my family but they denied me entry. Frantically, I cried out, "My wife and child have been shot! They might still be alive! Please, let me go in! Someone, anyone, please help them!"

Amidst the chaos of death and people fleeing in terror, my voice seemed to get lost in the cacophony. No one paid attention to my pleas. No one heard my cries for help. I felt desperate and utterly helpless, unable to reach anyone who could assist me. With each passing moment, hope slipped away, like the breath leaving the company of life. My heart shattered as I realized that my hopes of finding my wife and child alive were fading, leaving me in a state of profound grief and despair.

I sat huddled in a corner, consumed by fear and grief. The horrifying sounds of gunfire and explosions haunted me for three long days. As the days passed, I learned that all the terrorists had been killed, except for one who was captured alive. The toll of the tragedy was immense— many innocent lives were lost, including hotel staff, foreign as well as Indian guests, and even some police officials. What was their fault? Nothing. Yet, they fell victim to senseless violence. I could not comprehend who Murtaza and Gafoor were—we had never crossed paths, so, why did they take away Aditya and Aditi, and devastate my life?

On 29th November, in the afternoon, the lifeless bodies were brought out of the hotel. A pile of corpses lay before my eyes, and my heart raced as I searched for Aditi and Aditya amongst the deceased. The scene was filled with people desperately seeking news of their loved ones. Some found solace in knowing their relatives were safe, but many, like me, were only met with sorrow.

The burden of carrying the dead bodies of your family members on your shoulders is incomparable. Never did I imagine that I would have to face that day again, after already experiencing the loss of Prakash. My eyes felt like stone, my body was devoid of strength and my mind was shattered and overwhelmed with anxiety. I lacked the courage to see Aditi and Aditya's lifeless forms.

In the Hindu tradition, performing rituals is essential for a person to attain salvation. So, with the little courage that I had left, I went to the mortuary. My father-in-law was also there, which implied that my mother-in-law had also perished. In the wake of someone's passing, we often come to realize their true importance. I could not comprehend why my father-in-law apologized to me and hugged me tightly while tears streamed down his face.

Amidst the sorrowful cries and lifeless bodies, I began the heart-wrenching task of identifying Aditi's body, removing the shrouds from each face one by one. Deep down, I knew Aditi was gone, but a part of me still wished that she would miraculously be alive and well. However, reality does not always align with our desires.

Aditi's lifeless body lay before us, and the sight was heart-wrenching. Her once vibrant face now had a haunting shade of blue, and the impact of the bullet that had passed through her head left visible spots of blood. My instinctive response was to use my handkerchief to wipe the blood away but it had frozen, making it difficult to clean her face properly.

Without hesitation, I rushed outside and hurriedly returned with water to soak my handkerchief. Gently, I began to clean her face again, trying to restore some semblance of dignity to her lifeless form. The doctor standing nearby observed my efforts, and I could see the sadness in his eyes. Tears welled up in his eyes and his gaze reflected the shared sorrow that we both felt in the face of that tragic loss.

"What are you doing, Avinash?" asked my father-in-law, while keeping his hand on my shoulder.

"You don't know, Dad. Aditi always likes her face clean and…"

I kept silent while saying that sentence.

"Take care of yourself, Avinash. We have yet to find Aditya's and Sarika's dead bodies as well."

As we continued our search, we tragically discovered the lifeless body of my mother-in-law, who had suffered five strokes. The grief and sorrow seemed never-ending. We desperately looked for Aditya throughout the night but he was nowhere to be found. We combed through every corner of the hotel, hoping to find any sign of him but our efforts yielded no results.

Aditi's father, being influential and politically connected, secured permission for us to enter the hotel premises. The devastation left by the attack was evident— the walls were blackened by fire, and the lingering smoke filled the air. Despite our relentless search, there was no trace of Aditya.

Amidst the ruins, my eyes fell upon a half-lattice table, and beneath it lay one of Aditya's shoes. With trembling hands, I picked it up and saw that Aditya's cut and burnt leg were also inside the shoe. They were the same shoes that Aditi had lovingly designed for his birthday, with his initials inscribed on them. The sight was unbearable, and I could not hold back my emotions any longer. I let out a heart-wrenching scream, collapsed to the ground, and clung to his leg, sobbing uncontrollably in the face of such immense loss.

Those heartless individuals had mercilessly taken the life of my innocent child! The bomb blast had torn his tender body to shreds. As I looked around, I saw the horrifying aftermath of the attack—the bodies of numerous others were scattered in pieces, soaked in blood and burnt. Hands, legs and necks were strewn all around me—a grim reminder of the senseless violence that had transpired. I had never witnessed such a gruesome sight before, and the horror of it all overwhelmed me.

I continued to search frantically for any remains of Aditya's body, all the while screaming and crying in agony but I could only find his half-burnt leg and shoe. It was a devastating blow, leaving me shattered and unable to fathom the magnitude of my loss.

On that tragic day, I lit two pyres—one for Aditi and Aditya, and the other for myself. In a sense, I died along with them, as life seemed to strangle me with its unbearable grief. I was such an unfortunate father that I could not even perform the last rites of my beloved son. The weight of the sorrow and loss was too much to bear, and I felt like I was drowning in an ocean of pain and despair.

I had made a promise to Aditi that I would always protect her, and when Aditya was placed in my arms for the first time, I vowed to provide him with a good and secure life. But I could do nothing to prevent the tragedy that befell him—he was lost in the cruel tides of life.

Terrified, trembling and utterly helpless, I returned to my house and shut myself away from everyone. I sat alone, drowning in sorrow and unable to sleep for days on end. I would scream and seek refuge under the bed—feeling paralyzed by fear. My heart was filled with frustration and anger and I vented my emotions by repeatedly punching the wall for countless hours.

As time passed, days turned into weeks, weeks into months and three long months went by. The doorbell would ring daily but I lacked the strength to answer it or face the world outside. I did not know who came knocking at my door and then left. Everything appeared blurry through my tear-filled eyes. My body weakened, and my beard grew long—reflecting the toll that grief had taken on me.

One day, I glanced at myself in the mirror but I could not recognize the person staring back at me. I had become a mere shell of my former self, waiting only for death to come and take me away but even that seemed to elude me.

In the depths of my despair, while sleeping on my bed, someone gently stroked my head. Startled, I woke up, feeling frightened and vulnerable. It was my mother, sitting before me—her presence offering a glimmer of solace amidst the darkness that engulfed my life.

Smiling, she asked, "What happened, Avinash? Feeling defeated and helpless? Why are you sitting with your face turned away from life?"

Through my tears, I poured my heart out to my mother, by saying, "Mother, why did you take so long to come? What should I do now? To whom should I turn? First, you left, then Prakash, and now Aditi and Aditya—life has taken everything from me. My courage, strength and will to live have been shattered. Look at my fate, Mother. I have carried the lifeless bodies of many loved ones with these very hands. I have witnessed the passing of all of you with these eyes but I alone cannot find release from this torment. I feel breathless and overwhelmed with fear. Aditi and Aditya visit me in my dreams every night—constantly questioning what I have done for them. Aditya's screams haunt my ears."

"Aditi's face appears before me. She remains silent— always gazing at me intently. And there, in the corner, stands my mom, her tears flowing and observing me with countless unspoken queries. I yearn to wipe away her tears, lend an ear to her sorrows and embrace her tightly but I feel helpless and incapable of doing anything," I said and confided in my mother.

"Open the windows and doors of this house, Avinash. Let the sun, wind and noises from the outside world flood in. We are all distressed and saddened to see you in this state. Recognize the questions that Aditi had for you. You love her deeply, don't you? Transcend your sorrow and fear, and listen to her heart. Believe me, her voice will reach you," Mom said and vanished before my eyes, leaving behind a tender smile.

The doorbell rang, and someone knocked loudly on the door too.

That day, after almost four months, I opened the door. Father was standing in front of me. I kept looking at him for some time and stood wiping my tears.

"Stop rubbing your eyes. Get aside and let me enter the house. I am tired of travelling for so long," Father said.

The pain in his voice was visible but he had handled himself well.

On my doorstep, Jagdeep Singh was standing with his wife. Both were looking at me.

Mother asked me to open the windows and doors of the house. I came inside without closing the door.

"Haven't you found any city farther from this? It took two days to reach here. Now make tea for me—I am exhausted. And yes, your neighbours are also joining, so make two extra cups," Father spoke and scolded me.

I was making tea in the kitchen. Father opened the windows of the whole house and lit the lamp in the temple.

I made tea and put it on the dining table.

"Call Jagdeep. He is standing outside. I have been drinking tea at his house for the last four days," Father said.

By then, he had come inside the house. He hugged me. His eyes were moist. I requested him to sit and offered tea.

All three of us were calm and were drinking tea. My eyes fell on the lamp's flame in the temple, which fluttered in the strong wind.

"Don't worry, the flame of the lamp will not go out. The wind is strong, and there will be many struggles, but it will survive," Father said.

I started looking at him with teary eyes.

"I know you feel shattered and are in immense pain. You feel afraid too but you are not weak, Avinash. So much has happened, and you have been shutting yourself inside this house for many months. I called you so many times, but you didn't answer. Were you so upset with me that you did not even consider it worthy of sharing your sorrow with me? Thanks to Jagdeep's call to Sonali a few days back, we came to know about all this," Dad said, crying.

"Everything is over, Dad," I said and started crying and hugging him.

He kept pacifying me.

"We had thought that our son would become our greatest support and would take care of us during our old age. But he died in an extremist encounter in Kashmir. I was, am and always will be very proud of *Ishaan* as he died to save the honour of this nation but sadly, his life was compromised. I never thought that we would ever see the death of our son. We had nothing. We were disappointed and felt depressed. We tried committing suicide many times but we survived. And in the end, we came to terms with the situation. Do you know, Avinash, what is the most enormous sorrow of my life? Despite knowing everything, I could not save my son, nor could I do justice to his death. I wish I had dared," he confessed.

"Avinash, some people, whom you don't even know, and neither do they know you, ruin your life. At least you don't compromise with your situation and punish all those who have done wrong to you," he added.

I looked at him with astonishment. He smiled and said, "My words seem baseless, don't they?"

"It was a handful of extremists whom our police and army could hardly control. To kill and capture them, twice as many of our people were killed. Who do I take revenge on? The ones who died or the only ones who were caught and are now under the custody of police and the law?" I asked.

"Custody?" Jagdeep said and laughed out loud.

He continued, "I am well aware of the laws and systems in place here. I have witnessed them up close. Whatever transpired in the hotel that day, people know only what they need to know. When you got married and came to live here, it brought us immense joy. We no longer saw you as just a neighbour but as our son, Ishaan. I have observed and felt the deep love between you and Aditi, and witnessed the happiness you shared after Aditya's birth. The beautiful father-son bond you had with Aditya was something I greatly admired. I found myself reliving many moments of my life through yours. Your pain is unbearable, and you won't find peace until you seek justice for their deaths—whether it comes with your demise or by holding those responsible accountable. It's natural for a person to break down, feel suffocated, experience frustration, depression and even contemplate suicide when faced with such overwhelming anguish. Every moment, you may feel consumed by thoughts of self-destruction. After watching your loved ones being killed right before your eyes, how can you find solace? I consider you my son, and I do not want you to suffer as I still do. Ishaan often visits me in my dreams, asking, 'Dad, you knew everything. Why haven't you taken any action yet?' I have no answer for him—except my silence. Are you prepared to face such questions? Cease mourning their deaths and weeping in secrecy. Offer them respect—a tribute from a father to his son and from a husband to his wife. Seek justice against him and all those responsible for this tragedy. Do not make the mistake of believing that you are just an ordinary man. An ordinary man can also act fearlessly."

Saying this, he left to return home.

I could not sleep that night. Jagdeep Uncle's words flowed continuously in my mind and hit me constantly. Sitting on the bed, I looked at my phone's gallery. There were so many photographs of Aditi and Aditya. Then, I came across many photographs of the terrorist attack that day. I do not know how—maybe some button clicked. There were several screenshots of that day—of people, terrorists and most importantly, the one who shot Aditya. My blood boiled at the sight of his face. I kept looking at those pictures repeatedly and did not know when I had fallen asleep.

It was early morning. I was still sleepy, and Dad's favourite song's lyrics approached my ears.

Do not stop; you lose somewhere,

Shall go on thorns,

Will meet the shadow of Spring,

Oh, Walker…Oh, Traveller…Oh, Walker…Oh, Traveller…

Dad played that song loudly on the stereo and hummed along with it.

"Have you gotten up?" he asked.

I nodded.

"Let's get ready quickly—we must go somewhere."

Expressing surprise, I asked, "Where, Dad?"

"Is there a river or a big lake here? Take me there. A few last rituals and prayers are pending for Aditya and Aditi—I want to do them. Or, can you take me to Mumbai? I have heard that the hotel is next to the seashore. Can you take me there, please? I want to perform their last ritual there," Father said.

Nodding my head, I agreed.

We arrived in Mumbai and proceeded to purchase some essential items required for performing prayers. Eventually, we reached the hotel. As I made my way towards the seaside, I found myself unable to muster the courage to glance at the hotel. However, my dad kept his gaze fixed on the hotel for a prolonged period. Both of us stepped into the water, and my father began chanting *mantras*.

"Release them from your attachment by submerging their remains, Avinash. Only then will their souls find peace, and salvation shall be attained," Father advised.

I untied the cloth that covered the urn and poured the ashes into the sea. My mind was plagued with thoughts of how Aditya's soul would find rest. His lifeless body was never recovered, and I feared his spirit might still wander within that hotel, searching for Aditi, longing for me to come and rescue him. Perhaps, he still waited for my help.

"You know, Dad, on that dreadful day, he kept calling out to me, begging for assistance. He was in excruciating pain and kept asking, 'How long will it take for you to reach me?' But I failed—I couldn't reach him—I couldn't save him. He was murdered before my very eyes. His agonizing screams continue to echo in my ears and prevent me from finding any solace or sleep. A tempest rages within me. There's an inexplicable burning sensation and suffocation that won't let me live in peace, nor will it allow me to embrace death," I confessed, and my tears flowed freely.

Taking the phone out of my pocket, I showed Dad the picture of that terrorist and said, "He is the one who took Aditya away from us. His face haunts me constantly, by laughing and mocking me, as well as revelling in the brutal act of killing my innocent child…I feel utterly lost," I said, with tears streaming down my face.

I sat at my father's feet, wept and offered my prayers with folded hands.

"You are a great scholar, Dad. Do you have any solution that can bring peace to my child and me?" I asked hopefully.

He gazed at me and smiled gently, replying, "Give me your hand. There is still one more prayer left for the peace of another soul. Do you know who that soul is? It's you," he said.

I looked at him, taken aback by his words.

"I release you from all attachments, obligations and love. Life has continuously tested us with its most challenging trials, and each time, we've chosen silence and compromise. But enough is enough now. I want to hear the agonizing screams of that man, or whoever is responsible for the brutal murder of my grandson, daughter-in-law and you. I firmly believe that our God will not let this injustice go unpunished. Regardless of what the world may say, I am certain that this man is still alive. I yearn to witness the tormenting end of the one who has inflicted so much sorrow upon us. Turn your pain into strength, transform your inner anger into an unyielding shield and let your tears become your weapon. I know you have always loved me more than Prakash, and for that love, I beseech you to promise me that you will pay tribute to Aditi and Aditya. By doing so, I can be proud of you and find peace in my heart before departing from this world."

"I release you from all responsibilities towards me, from all obligations and affections. Whether you return or not, my only expectation from you now is to punish those devils as fiercely as you can. This is your purpose now, and I, Kripa Shankar Tripathi, your father, forbid you from leaving this world until you fulfil what I ask of you. If death is inevitable, then grant me one final favour as your father—speak to me once more. I will forever pray for the peace of your soul. Promise me, Avinash, that one day I will be proud of you," Dad said.

Now one last purpose of life had been found.

"I promise, Dad," I said.

It was a promise by a son to his father and a father to his son.

Chapter 3

Varanasi Returns

Bangalore, 2008

(The doorbell rang.)

"Hello, Avinash," Jagdeep Uncle replied.

"Can I come in?" I asked.

"Yes, of course. How are you doing? Has your father gone back to Varanasi? Please come in and sit," he replied.

"Who are you?" I asked, looking into his eyes.

"What kind of question is that, Avinash? Don't you know who I am?" he asked with a surprised look on his face.

"I know, but I want to know what I don't know," I replied.

"Either Aditi or I always spoke minimally about my dad and Sonali. How did you contact them? Did you get their contact details and then ask Dad to come here? What do you know about the hotel attack that is unknown to others?" I asked.

"Oh, that's a very petty thing, Avinash. In today's world, finding someone's information is easy," he replied, ignoring my question.

"This is not what I asked for, Jagdeep Uncle."

Forwarding my phone's screen towards him, I asked, "Do you know him? Is he dead or alive after this attack? Can you help me trace him?" I showed him the picture of that terrorist who got clicked.

Looking into my eyes, he asked in a hoarse voice, "What do you want to do?"

"Neither Aditi nor Aditya—I cannot bear to confront the thought of either of them being gone. Aditya's agonizing cries still haunt my ears, and I yearn for solace in their absence. The image of Aditi's lifeless body continues to suffocate me— leaving me gasping for air. I long to find peace and breathe freely again. Even when I close my eyes, their tear-streaked faces linger, imploring me for help. I desperately wish to assist them."

"My heart weighs heavily with the burden of grief, and I yearn to lighten its load. I am determined to hold those responsible for Aditya's untimely demise accountable for their actions. Each person involved—anyone who caused his suffering will have to answer his cries. In his final moments, Aditya's words, 'Miss you, Dad,' still echo in my mind. I ache to respond, 'I miss you too, my son.'"

"I was Aditya's hero and Aditi's pillar of belief. Death is an unavoidable reality, and I am certain that I will reunite with them, someday. Though I am unsure of the how, when and in what form, I wish that whenever that day comes, they will feel proud of me, radiate happiness, wear constant smiles and dwell in eternal peace."

"There are those who must face the consequences— not only him but all who bear responsibility for the tragedies that occurred. Perhaps no one can comprehend my anguish as deeply as you can. This is my tribute to them, and I believe you can assist me, which is why I am here. I have made my decision, and I am resolute in it!" I declared.

"Ishaan, who served in the army, was stationed on the POK border when he reached out to me three days prior to his untimely demise. He had stumbled upon a substantial lead concerning the leader of a highly prominent and active terrorist group. This group was planning a colossal attack on the Indian border, intending to bomb several locations in Kashmir. Shockingly, the conspiracy involved prominent figures and politicians from both sides of the conflict. Their nefarious intentions extended beyond an attack—they had sinister plans to assassinate officials and leaders involved in peace talks. Their ultimate goal was to seize control of the region of Kashmir under POK."

Ishaan had a crucial piece of evidence—a recorded conversation that exposed their plans. He dutifully reported the matter to his superior officer but regrettably, it was not taken seriously. He was merely instructed to monitor any further developments and relay information to the authorities. Meanwhile, the terrorist group proceeded with the implementation of their deadly schemes while our forces were instructed to wait and observe passively."

"On the day of his demise, in the early-morning hours, Ishaan reached out to me once more, expressing grave concern over a life-threatening situation that had arisen for him and the soldiers at his post. He disclosed the cold and indifferent response he received from his superiors regarding this alarming matter," lamented Jagdeep Uncle.

"I served as an undercover agent for the intelligence agency of our country. On that fateful day, Ishaan entrusted me with several photographs and an audio recording. Without delay, I rushed to our department to report this critical intelligence. Unfortunately, by the time any substantial action could be taken, Kashmir was engulfed in a devastating barrage of explosions. More than 20 army posts were targeted, resulting in the tragic loss of hundreds of soldiers and thousands of innocent lives, including my beloved son, who also perished in the horrifying attack. Among the victims were numerous individuals who sought nothing but peace."

Following the calamity, a blame game ensued, and Ishaan was unjustly labelled a traitor due to his sharing of sensitive army information with an undercover agent. As a consequence, the army initiated an investigation against both my son and me, while the intelligence department disowned me completely. This led to a gruelling five-year trial, during which I repeatedly questioned the actions of the national security agencies. I sought answers regarding the actions taken by that senior official when Ishaan presented irrefutable evidence of the impending danger. Instead of addressing the actual threat, this official craftily evaded accountability by laying blame on my son and me, accusing us of insensitivity and mishandling critical and vital information."

"I was unjustly sentenced to life imprisonment and thrown into jail under false charges of jeopardizing the security of our country and exploiting crucial information for personal gain. It was a harrowing ordeal, and it took nearly six long months for the truth to finally surface—revealing the involvement of the army officer with the terrorists and their connection to the POK. Consequently, I was exonerated, and my physical body was released from the confines of the prison on that day. However, my spirit, my happiness and my very life continue to remain imprisoned, even to this day," Jagdeep sombrely concluded.

"Do you know who that official was, Avinash?" he asked.

He opened his phone, placed a photograph before my eyes and said, "*Murtaza Arzai*, the name of terror today!"

"Is it not him?" I asked surprisingly.

"The only difference is that he is wearing an Indian army uniform in your photograph," I said.

"Yes, he is the one," Jagdeep Uncle replied.

"I realized that he possessed valuable information about the person I sought and could aid me in achieving my objectives. Is he still alive? How can I locate him? I am determined to track down this man," I inquired, my voice filled with anger and resolve.

"Do you wish to find him?" Jagdeep Uncle asked, a smile playing on his lips.

"He is not the one we seek. The mystery surrounding the identity of Murtaza Arzai is perplexing, as multiple individuals bearing that name seem to exist, which makes it difficult to ascertain who the real person is. Allegedly, two individuals with that name have already met their demise—one at the hands of the Indian intelligence and the other by the Vietnam police. However, shockingly, he resurfaced during the Mumbai attack and was spotted at the hotel. While there are no official reports of his death during the recent Mumbai hotel attack, the police have managed to obtain numerous video clips and photographs of him. Their ongoing investigation aims to unravel the circumstances of his escape from the hotel, and it is evident that he is still alive, or rather, one more individual claiming to be him is still living," he further explained.

"One more of him?" I asked surprisingly.

"What do you mean by this? He could be only one but not so many—I don't understand," I said.

"He is an illusion, wielding the power to instil fear, brutality and chaos, thereby perpetuating a worldwide atmosphere of panic. Though he exists, the true extent of his presence remains an enigma. Some speculate that he may have cloned himself multiple times, while others suggest he is one of the quadruplet brothers. According to international agencies, two have been reported dead but uncertainty shrouds the number of surviving individuals claiming to be Murtaza Arzai. The crux of the matter is that only Murtaza Arzai himself knows the identity of the real Murtaza Arzai," Jagdeep Uncle explained.

"Avinash, what you seek to accomplish is akin to finding a drop in the vast ocean, and demands arduous preparation. You must become an unwavering force, impervious to pain, affection or emotion and a formidable presence none can hinder. Transform yourself into a relentless killing machine, striking fear into anyone who dares to stand in your way, even causing death itself to tremble at the sight of you. To destroy a volcano, you must become a fire fiercer than it. Your sole focus must be revenge. Can you do it?" he questioned.

I gazed at them for a moment and then spoke firmly, "I have nothing left to lose, so what is there to fear? All those who once loved me are no more—thus leaving behind no attachments or affection. My father has already performed my last rituals, and as a dead person, I have no fear of death. Admittedly, I am weak and have lost all courage, but my circumstances have forged an inner strength within me. Although my heart is burdened with pain, I have ceased crying. However, there will come a day when I will cry for the last time, and on that day, Murtaza Arzai will be at my mercy, begging for his life. I will shed tears while paying homage to Aditi and my son, Aditya."

Turning to Jagdeep Uncle, I implored, "You can assist, train and guide me to achieve my goal. Let the father in both of us seek justice for our children—me for Aditya and you for Ishaan. We both yearn for relief from this excruciating pain, and peace will evade us until Murtaza meets his end." With that, I humbly knelt before him, making my request.

The tears flowing from his eyes kept falling on my forehead.

"I feel your pain, Son. I know how difficult it is to live with this suffocation."

Affectionately stroking my head, he said, "A determined man can never be defeated. I will make you that capable, by which you can face any situation. Get up, wipe your tears and start walking on the path of your strong determination. Let's do it," he said.

The following day, both of us headed to Malleswaram, and I witnessed Jagdeep Uncle adorned in a business suit for the first time. He looked sharp and sophisticated in black attire. Departing from home in my car, we reached Malleswaram, where we took an auto for a short distance before switching to a rickshaw that took us to our destination—the Kadu Malleshwara Temple. This 17th-century A.D. Hindu temple is dedicated to Lord Shiva and is located in the Malleshwara area of Bengaluru, Karnataka. The name Kadu alludes to the dense greenery surrounding the temple.

"Let us seek the blessings of Lord Shiva," Jagdeep Uncle suggested, and we both stood before the deity with folded hands.

Suddenly, a voice reached our ears, asking, "How did you remember God today?"

We turned around and found a man standing behind us, towering at about seven feet tall. He was clad in priest's robes, but his appearance did not quite match that of a typical priest. With a warm smile, he beckoned us to follow him, and we complied. Jagdeep Uncle seemed to sense my curiosity and advised me to refrain from asking questions and stay focused while walking.

As we trailed behind him, we ventured into a forested area, where an old building in ruins came into view. There, the man offered Jagdeep Uncle a drink of water, pouring it into two glasses from a nearby pot. Then, he turned to me and casually inquired about my well-being, and addressed me by name. I was astounded that someone I had never met before knew my name.

"Don't be astonished. You may not know me, but I am familiar with every aspect of your life," he divulged, revealing his profound knowledge of me.

"Well, do tell, Jagdeep. It's evident that you didn't come here to seek God's blessings, and apart from Avinash, you don't know anyone else in this place. It appears that after many years, you've come to your friend with an exceptionally extraordinary purpose," the man addressed Jagdeep with an air of understanding.

"I want you to train Avinash and mould him into an unbeatable soldier," Jagdeep Uncle stated, making his request.

The man chuckled heartily in response, almost mocking the idea. "You want me to turn him into a soldier who cannot be defeated?" he said, continuing to laugh scornfully.

"Yes, make him a soldier who is invincible," Jagdeep Uncle reiterated, undeterred by the man's laughter.

The man's laughter eventually subsided as he looked at Avinash thoughtfully. "Very well then, let's see what can be done," he said, his expression now serious.

Then a solemn silence enveloped us, and Riyaz Ahmed spoke earnestly, "I don't teach anyone without a clear purpose, and any reason must align with the benefit of my nation. I'm sorry, Jagdeep but I don't understand what led you here. Have you forgotten the oath we both took together when we joined the Indian intelligence?"

"'I, the soldier of this nation, will always uphold its pride and honour, whether in service or beyond. We shall forever serve in the best interest of this nation, setting aside our agendas.' This oath remains unchanged, even after retirement or in the face of death. Isn't that true, Jagdeep?" he continued.

"He neither has a clear purpose nor is he a soldier of my nation. And you want me to train him?" Riyaz Ahmed said, his tone reflecting his concern and disapproval.

"Gentleman, I can only extend my deepest sympathies to you and understand your predicament. I know that you, too, have suffered a loss in that dreadful hotel attack. Please consider it as the darkest of dreams in your life, try to move forward, take care of your remaining family members, and strive to find happiness. I will pray to Lord Shiva for your peace, well-being, and contentment," he kindly addressed me.

As I gazed into his eyes, I replied, "Yes, you are absolutely right. Who am I to expect any assistance from you? Why should you help me in any way?"

After a brief pause, I took a deep breath and continued, "But, Sir, what truly defines a nation? Is it not its citizens? They are the lifeblood that keeps it alive—propelling it to thrive. Despite the countless sacrifices made by our soldiers who stand vigilantly at our borders, risking their lives daily to safeguard us, we still face threats from those who seek to harm us. I am certain that you know many such soldiers and have trained them as well," I earnestly expressed my thoughts.

I leant forward, my eyes burning with intensity. "I am one of those citizens. I have witnessed the horrifying reality of terrorism up close. I watched helplessly as my wife and child were torn away from me, and I heard the heartless laughter of the man responsible for their agony. I will never forget that man and his boastful confession of killing numerous innocent souls. My precious son, my flesh and blood, was left screaming for my protection. When I reached the hotel, what I found will haunt me forever—a half-amputated leg and one shoe, the remnants of my beloved son," I recounted with a heavy heart.

Taking a deep breath, my resolve unwavering, I continued, "The man who robbed me of everything, who callously snuffed out the lives of so many innocent souls, will face the consequences. He will pay with every drop of his blood for every life he took. I don't need to prove myself to anyone. As a father, I seek to honour my son's memory by extracting every last ounce of retribution from his murderer, and I will relish the sound of his painful screams."

My determination to seek justice burned fiercely, fuelled by the memories of the ones I loved most, whose lives were unjustly cut short by an evil hand.

I held my gaze, unwavering, as I delivered my final words. "I have made my decision. Whether you choose to assist me or not is entirely up to you. But understand this—I will not falter in achieving my goal. Somewhere, my son is still waiting for me, and when we are reunited, I want to see pride and happiness in his eyes, not sorrow. I bid you farewell. Let's go, Jagdeep Uncle," I declared, turning to leave.

Curiosity got the better of Riyaz, and he inquired, "Whom do you intend to kill? Whom did you identify in the Mumbai hotel attack?"

"Murtaza Arzai," I replied firmly.

At my response, Riyaz burst into loud laughter, unable to contain his amusement. "You talk about killing someone whom the intelligence and the armies of not just India but many other countries have failed to locate!" he scoffed.

Still laughing, he picked up a large stone and threw it towards me—striking my chest. The impact of the rock caused me to moan in pain but my determination remained unshaken. I knew that my path ahead would be filled with obstacles and challenges but nothing could deter me from seeking justice for my beloved son and countless others who had suffered at the hands of Murtaza Arzai.

"The one seeking to eliminate Murtaza Arzai must possess not just speed, intellect and strength but also cruelty, lethality and an ability to endure pain without flinching. Today, you were unable to catch a stone thrown swiftly at you. Your training shall be considered complete only when you can seize a bullet fired from a gun with your bare hands. However, you must not question anything during your training. You have until 4 a.m. tomorrow to attend to your affairs and meet whomever you wish. But starting tomorrow, your life will belong to me. This is the deal," declared Riyaz with authority.

With a heart full of emotions, I humbly bowed down to Riyaz and departed from his presence.

"Avinash, life has granted you an opportunity, and you mustn't let it slip away in vain. Riyaz's acceptance of your proposal is nothing short of a blessing. He is like the fire that refines you—the more you endure, the more you shine. This is where the most critical part of your journey begins," Jagdeep Uncle conveyed with utmost seriousness and wisdom.

As I returned home, the realization dawned upon me that *that* night could very well be my last night in that place. Packing my belongings, I understood that there might be no turning back. My mind was a whirlwind of emotions—a strange mix of happiness, restlessness and fear. As I lay down to sleep, the clock read 2:00 a.m. Suddenly, the doorbell rang, and I cautiously opened the door to find a young boy, approximately 15 years old, standing before me.

"We must leave. Otherwise, we will be late," he said calmly.

Surprised, I hesitated for a moment and asked, "Who are you?"

His reply was swift and firm, "You were told not to ask any questions. Just follow me."

Without further ado, I gathered my bags and followed him outside. The boy gave me a once-over, a hint of a smile crossing his face and he gestured for me to keep moving.

As we reached the temple, the boy directed me to take a bath and don the clothes that he provided. He reiterated the instruction not to ask any questions, and I complied obediently. Together, we ventured deep into the heart of the dense forest, guided only by the mysterious path ahead.

Suddenly, a familiar voice called out my name—it was Riyaz Ahmed, dressed in the same attire as me. He pointed to a tree in front of us with a rope hanging from it and asked, "Do you see that tree, Avinash?"

I turned to look, and to my surprise, Sarvnaam had joined us as well. Riyaz continued, "Climb the tree, tie the rope around your feet and hang upside down. Ensure that it's secure, as any slack could lead to your head exploding."

I was taken aback by the sudden and strange request, about to ask questions but the boy, Sarvnaam, bluntly cut me off, saying, "No one questions our Master."

Despite my hesitation and fear of heights, I tried to explain that I did not know how to climb trees but Riyaz left and instructed Sarvnaam to teach me. Under the tree, I inquired, "So, your name is Sarvnaam?"

"We'll get to know each other later," he replied, gesturing towards the tree. "First, watch this."

He swiftly climbed the tree, tied himself with the rope and began swinging while emitting loud, joyful and amusing sounds.

"It's your turn now," he said and called out to me.

Summoning all my strength, I ran towards the tree and made attempts to climb it. However, I failed repeatedly, injuring myself badly with blood seeping from my hands and feet. Despite the pain, I refused to give up and kept trying.

Observing me closely, Sarvnaam asked, "Do you know why you're struggling to climb?"

He then imparted wisdom, explaining that I needed to maintain a balance between enthusiasm and composure, with a focus on technique and calculation. With his guidance, I successfully climbed the tree and felt a sense of accomplishment as I reached the top.

"Excellent," Sarvnaam complimented, acknowledging my progress.

"Now tie your feet with the rope. The one who can never deceive or let you down is yourself. Have faith and believe in your abilities. Secure the rope well and relax your body. Let go of all your fears, close your eyes and descend gracefully," Sarvnaam instructed.

Initially hesitant, I eventually followed his guidance and floated down from the tree, feeling a rush of sensations as my feet touched the ground. Though disoriented at first, Sarvnaam reassured me and advised me to relax and let my hands hang freely.

As I adjusted to my surroundings, Sarvnaam gave me a new task. "Stay like this until this afternoon, and then join us at the temple for lunch. I'm sure you'll feel hungry by then," he said before walking away.

However, as I opened my eyes, I realized that I was utterly alone. Feeling confused and frustrated, I shouted after him, "Hey, wait! I don't know how to get down from here. Where are you going, leaving me behind?" But he did not turn back.

Struggling to make sense of his cryptic instructions, I attempted to find a way to descend from the tree. Around 20 feet off the ground, I flailed about in agony, shouting in despair as I desperately tried to untie myself. After much struggle and fear, I finally managed to release myself from the rope but unfortunately, I fell harshly on the ground, inflicting severe injuries upon myself. My shoulder dislocated, and a sharp wooden object pierced my back, leaving me immobile and writhing in pain.

Lying there, crying and sobbing helplessly, I suddenly became aware of someone watching me. It was Sarvnaam.

"We all have to carry our burdens," he declared sternly.

"You're fine. Get up and walk," he encouraged.

Though feeling incredibly angry, I mustered every bit of strength and managed to push myself up, dragging my injured body as I began to make my way towards the temple.

Riyaz was calmly having his lunch and was seemingly unperturbed by my condition. Thirsty and in need of water, I urgently requested someone for help but my pleas fell on deaf ears. A pitcher of water was conveniently placed nearby but nobody seemed to acknowledge my needs.

Growing frustrated and angry, I raised my voice but still, no one paid attention to me. With trembling hands, I reached for a clay glass nearby and filled it with water. Just as I was about to take a sip, Riyaz unexpectedly picked up a stone and hurled it at the glass, thus shattering it into pieces.

I sat in a corner with my emotions overflowing as I expressed my frustration. "What kind of behaviour is this? Are you here to train me or kill me? Can't you see that I am hurt and in pain? Instead of helping, you both are torturing me!"

Riyaz remained unmoved. He finished his meal before speaking sternly to me—"Are you worried about some bruises, scratches, blood and pain? Nothing serious happened to you. You are alive, breathing and fine. What more could you ask for?"

He continued by saying, "Sitting here and shouting won't get you anywhere. If you want to leave, the door is right there. But if you choose to stay, don't expect anyone else to help you. The only person who can truly help you is yourself. Don't let your pain and situation become your weakness. In times of war, a soldier may get shot and suffer wounds but they keep fighting until their last breath. Riyaz Ahmed only knows such soldiers. So, stop the drama and get up. Rise in a way that you will never fall again."

Finally, he emphasized, **"You are alive, until you die!"**

His words resonated deeply within me, infusing a renewed sense of determination and vitality. I held him in high regard, and at that moment, my pain and injuries seemed to fade away. Without a second thought, I stood up and respectfully addressed him, "Master, what is your next instruction? I am ready."

With a gentle smile, he approached me and took hold of my hand. Skilfully, he reset my dislocated shoulder, relieving me of the intense pain. He then advised me to nourish myself and get ample rest, preparing for the challenges that lay ahead on the following day.

"Sarvnaam, please make sure he receives proper food and medicine for his wounds," he instructed, before leaving.

I felt a sense of gratitude for Sarvnaam's care and the transformational experience under Riyaz's guidance. My resolve was stronger than ever before, and I was eager to face whatever trials awaited me in the pursuit of my mission.

The next morning brought a new day and a new version of myself. My task was to become a skilled soldier who could handle the worst situations. Riyaz Ahmed was a master trainer, known for his unorthodox and rigorous training methods, and he was determined to transform me into a formidable fighter.

Days were filled with tough and rigorous training, coupled with healthy food to help me gain strength. I climbed trees, tying and untying myself countless times until I could make a perfect landing. I was put on ice, made to run for miles barefoot, and endured physical and mental challenges that awaited.

Every day began early in the morning with waking up before dawn to run for miles, pushing myself beyond limits that I thought were not possible. I lifted weights, did push-ups, sit-ups and other exercises, which were designed to build muscle and endurance. Despite the aches and pains, I refused to give up, thus pushing myself harder each day.

In the afternoons, the focus shifted to martial arts training. Riyaz was a master of several different styles and techniques, and he taught me everything that he knew. I practised punches, kicks, blocks and parries until my movements were fluid and precise. He taught me how to disarm an opponent, how to use weapons and how to fight in close quarters.

But Riyaz's training did not stop there. He also trained me in shooting targets and taught me how to handle guns and aim accurately. I spent hours at the shooting range, firing shot after shot until my aim was perfect.

Weeks turned into months, and I transformed into someone whom I could never have imagined myself to be. My muscles grew larger, my reflexes became quicker and I became a deadly fighter as Riyaz had promised.

However, Riyaz knew that training the body was only half the battle. He also worked on training my mind, by teaching me how to focus, control my emotions and remain calm under pressure.

The training continued for months, and I emerged stronger, faster and more powerful. I became a master of martial arts, a deadly shooter and a fighter who was impossible to defeat. Thanks to Riyaz's unorthodox and rigorous training methods, I was now prepared to handle any situation that could come my way.

One morning, I arrived at the forest well on time, but Riyaz and Sarvnaam were nowhere to be found. I waited for a while, but they did not show up, so, I went to the temple to look for them. I searched everywhere, but there was no sign of Riyaz. I even checked his room, but he was nowhere to be found.

Just then, Sarvnaam entered the temple carrying bundles of garlands. "Where is Rizvan, I mean the Master?" I asked him.

Sarvnaam raised his neck and pointed towards the dome of the temple. "He was changing the flag on the dome."

Soon he got down and said smiling, "Get ready and come fast. Today is Goddess Durga's *Havan*."

I quickly got ready and joined Rizvan near the *Havan Kund*, where he was preparing for the worship. Many other priests and devotees were also present. I whispered to Sarvnaam, "Is today a special day?"

"*Navratri* starts from today, and prayers are performed here for nine whole days," he replied.

Rizvan gestured for me to sit, and the chanting of *mantras* began. I sat with folded hands and closed my eyes but a few moments later, Aditi appeared in front of my eyes. She used to fast for the entire span of nine days during *Navratri*, and Aditya and I were always expected to get up early and be ready for the prayers, which we did not like that much. Aditi would scold us almost every day for being late, but I loved it, as she was the only one who scolded us rightly and loved us a lot.

"Today, you got up so early and got ready for the prayers," Aditi's voice echoed in my mind, and I smiled.

Suddenly, the conch shell blew, and my eyes opened. I realized that I had been dreaming, and tears flowed from my eyes.

Riyaz gave me a sacrament. "So, will we start the training after nine days now?" I asked.

"Your training is complete now. You are prepared to approach your target," declared Riyaz.

I was taken aback by the sudden realization that my training had come to an end. "How can I achieve my goal without your guidance?" I asked, feeling uncertain.

"Avinash, we are all solitary warriors, fighting our own battles. I have imparted what I can, and now it is time for you to move forward with confidence and strength. But don't worry. Whenever you need my assistance, it will find you," Riyaz assured me.

His words filled me with both trepidation and empowerment. "But how will you know if I achieve my goal or whether I am alive or dead?" I inquired, still unsure.

"I never abandon my soldiers, Avinash. As I mentioned before, I will be aware of every step you take. I will know when you require my aid and be there to support you. However, before you depart, there is one last thing I want to impress upon you. I have never taught my soldiers to die. Even if death seems inevitable, a soldier must fight, vanquish the enemy and meet their fate courageously. Never forget this," he commanded.

"I won't forget it," I vowed.

"Good. Now, this is my final instruction for you, or you can consider it a test to evaluate what you have learned," Riyaz stated, concluding our training on a powerful note.

"Your wish is my command," I replied, ready to face any challenges that lay ahead.

Riyaz continued, "Mohammad Ilyas Bakari is a man from a highly influential and politically powerful family. He may be known as a successful businessman and politician but he is deeply involved in major cross-border smuggling and suspected of engaging in various terrorist activities within the country. Despite numerous police inquiries, he has always managed to elude justice due to his brother's political connections and influence. Our sources indicate that he is an active member of the Free Kashmir Mission (FKM), a terrorist organization that recruits and radicalizes youth, promotes drug use and carries out targeted assassinations. Bakari is also believed to be a significant drug supplier in the country and is known to operate various training camps in and around Jammu."

Riyaz paused for a moment and then continued, "Moreover, he has a dispute with the FKM chief and is currently blackmailing the organization. Aware of the danger he poses, Bakari has been in hiding in India with his brother's support for nearly a year. Due to the valuable information, which he could provide, we must locate Bakari as soon as possible."

Curiosity and determination filled me as I asked Riyaz, "How will I find Bakari? Where is he?"

Riyaz looked at me with a mysterious smile, "Finding Bakari is part of your final assignment, Avinash. Use everything you have learned, rely on your instincts, and trust in your training. You will receive the necessary information at the right time, and I will be there to guide you if required. Remember, you are now a force to be reckoned with. Go out there and make us proud."

"You haven't seen your father for a long time, have you? It's time to return to Varanasi. My trusted associate will meet you there and provide you with a clue about Bakari. Get ready to leave. Jagdeep is waiting for you outside," Riyaz replied.

"May I ask you a question?" I requested.

"Of course, you can ask as many questions as you wish. Tell me what's on your mind," Riyaz replied.

"I have only one question. Why did you agree to help me?" I asked.

"Parents see their lives in their children. They live, cherish and do anything for their children that they couldn't do or achieve in their own lives. They nurture their children and watch them grow, hoping that their kids will see them off peacefully at their last moment. Witnessing one's children's deaths before them is the heaviest burden a parent can bear. You witnessed your son's death before your eyes. I may not be a father, but I can empathize with how my father was always worried about me and feared not seeing me alive the next day. I saw their daily uneasiness, anxiety and nervousness for me. A father never speaks much but quietly works to raise his family and silently leaves this world. I feel your pain as a father—your helplessness, suffocation and burden. I only want to alleviate that burden if I can," Riyaz said.

Tears welled up in my eyes upon hearing his heartfelt words.

"Don't let them fall," Riyaz thundered. "Soldiers do not cry. You are my soldier."

I tried to hold back my tears—not wanting to disappoint my mentor.

"Now, go and fulfil your promise," he said.

"May I ask one more thing?" I asked. Riyaz nodded in agreement.

"I have never seen a Muslim serve as a priest in a Hindu temple before, except for you," I said.

"A soldier has no religion. My religion is my country, and I do whatever suits its safety and happiness. Yes, I am a Muslim, and my religion has taught me equality and respect for all religions, love for everyone, to help others and live a dignified life. And this is what every true Muslim does and will continue to do," Riyaz explained with pride in his eyes and honour in his voice.

That day, my respect for him grew even more. I touched his feet, seeking permission to leave.

As I turned to go, he said, "Avinash, have no mercy. Murtaza Arzai must meet a painful death. He should beg you for death and suffer until his last breath."

Varanasi, June 2009.

Verse 1:

Walking down these streets,

Where once I knew every face,

But now they all seem strange,

And I feel so out of place.

Chorus:

I am unknown in my own city,

Maybe this is the last meeting,

With this place that I used to call home,

But now I feel so alone.

Verse 2:

My life was once so full,

In the lap of my dear father,

But now he's gone and I'm left,

With this emptiness that lingers longer.

Chorus:

I am unknown in my own city,

Maybe this is the last meeting,

With this place that I used to call home,

But now I feel so alone.

Bridge:

All these memories flood my mind,

Of moments we shared so divine,

But now I must say goodbye,

To this city and my father's side.

Chorus:

I am unknown in my own city,

Maybe this is the last meeting,

With this place that I used to call home,

But now I feel so alone.

Outro:

Farewell to this place I've known,

I'll carry these memories on my own,

But now it's time to move along,

To new places where I belong.

The phone rang, and I answered it with a short "Hello."

A voice on the other end said, "Come and taste Kashmiri apples at 6:00 p.m. today. See you at the *ghat*."

The call abruptly ended, leaving me wondering who the mysterious caller was. I suspected that it was probably one of Riyaz's men, as he had given me a code to identify them.

As I strolled around the city, memories of my childhood flooded my mind. I reminisced about my favourite evening spots with friends and the delicious food we used to enjoy.

As the sun set, I arrived at the *ghat*, where several priests were preparing for the grand prayer ceremony of the holy river, the Ganga.

The sight of the priests offering prayers with drums and huge lamps drew in thousands of devotees daily. My mother used to bring me there to witness that magnificent spectacle often. Aditi also wanted to join us but she never got the chance.

Suddenly, a loud voice interrupted my thoughts. "You have come to Banaras after a long time. After the prayers, you must take the *prasad*," a priest said.

I turned around to see a portly man in his priestly attire, beckoning me. After the prayers, he invited me to ride a boat to the middle of the river. I asked him who he was and how he recognized me but he just smiled and said, "Concentrate on your work."

He handed me a bundle and asked if I knew how to row a boat. Feeling confused, I returned to the *ghat* and went to my lodge. I closed all the windows and doors properly and opened the bundle. Inside was the *prasad* and a piece of paper that caught my attention.

I was taken aback by what was printed and written on the paper. The face and name on the paper belonged to the one who had destroyed my family and me—Mohammad Ilyas Rizvi, Bakari's brother. The order for me was clear—"Where is Bakari? It is only known to his brother Ilyas Rizvi. You have time till tomorrow. Remember, don't leave any evidence behind. You will need some weapons, which shall reach you tomorrow morning. The paper with the message that came with the *prasad* should not be thrown away but can be burnt."

The next morning, was *the day*!

A rush of memories flooded my mind as I stood before the towering multi-storeyed building. I had been there before—many years ago. It was the office of Bhairav and Rizvi, the same place where my dad had been mercilessly beaten. The mere sight of the building sent shivers down my spine as I recalled the trauma that had unfolded there.

My heart raced as I approached the entrance, feeling hesitant and unsure of what I would find inside. The imposing structure loomed over me as a stark reminder of the violence and fear that had taken hold of my family all those years ago.

But there was no fear today. I pushed open the heavy glass doors and stepped inside.

As I approached the receptionist, she greeted me with a warm smile and asked how she could assist me.

"I'm here to see Mohammad Ilyas Rizvi," I said.

"I'm sorry but Mr. Rizvi doesn't typically meet visitors without an appointment. And it appears that no meetings are scheduled for him today," she replied politely.

Realizing the potential difficulty in my situation, I explained my circumstances to the receptionist. "I understand, but I'm only in town for a few hours, and I don't want to miss the opportunity of seeing my dear old friend. Would it be possible for you to let him know that Avinash is here to return something to him?"

The receptionist looked concerned and suggested that I wait while she checked with Mr. Rizvi's office. Within seconds, I was surrounded by several imposing bodyguards. "Oh, well, Rizvi Sir is keen to meet you. He is going to be here at any moment. Meanwhile, these people will take care of you properly. Please take him to the meeting place. Please *enjoy* the hospitality," she said, smiling.

As we made our way to the sixth floor, I could not help but feel intimidated by the silent presence of the bodyguards. But once we arrived at the meeting place, I was surprised to find only a table and four chairs in the otherwise empty room. The bodyguards maintained their stoic composure but I could sense that they were highly alert.

I intentionally remained calm, continuously looking at the door and waiting for him.

A clear sound of shoes knocking against the floor was nearing me. That was him—*Rizvi* and of course, *Bhairav,* accompanying him.

"Hello, Avinash," Rizvi said with a smirk.

"Oh, I hope all is well with you. You look so fit and sturdy," he said in a teasing voice.

Bhairav was staring at me. I did not say a word. I knew that it was going to be a fight to the death.

Bhairav's face contorted with anger as he spoke. "Have you forgotten what happened last time?" he asked, and his voice sounded tense.

"I find it difficult to be around you people without feeling disgusted. Does your father know you are here?"

Rizvi gestured to his bodyguards, and they slowly began to close in on me.

"I can't see the fear in your eyes today," he said.

"You are up to something. Maybe it's revenge or something else but poor boy, why have you come here all alone again? I will be despondent to kill you," he laughed out loudly.

Hitting his fist hard on the table, he asked, "Why the hell have you come here?"

"Where is your brother, *Bakari*?" I asked.

He looked at me and seemed shocked.

"*Bakari*? How do you even know my brother's name? What do you want from him?" he asked angrily.

"This is not my only question. Can I request you to listen to all my questions and reply patiently before you die, today? I know you are thinking, why, how and how dare I? But that's okay. You don't deserve to know, nor am I in the mood to tell you," I replied.

"Why did you kill my brother?" I asked firmly.

"How dare you? You and your father should have been killed that day with your brother. That was a huge mistake but never mind, today is a good day to give you a dog's death," Bhairav said and charged at me.

I held his hand and twisted and cracked his bones. I held his neck and it broke. In seconds, he was on the ground, dead. Riyaz had taught me well, and with just a few gentle touches, anyone could be put to death—and I used the knowledge well.

The first bodyguard lunged at me, but I quickly sidestepped and delivered a powerful kick to his ribs. He fell to the ground, writhing in pain. I quickly turned to face the next attacker, and the fight was on.

For the next few minutes, I fought with all my might. I dodged punches and kicks, ducked under swinging arms and delivered bone-crunching blows to my opponents. The bodyguards kept coming but I was unstoppable. I became a blurry movement that took down my attackers one by one.

Rizvi watched in horror as his men fell to my feet under the influence of my fists. He knew that he had underestimated me that day. But he could not let me walk away from there alive. He pulled out a gun and aimed it at my head. But before he could fire, I lunged forward and knocked the gun out of his hand. With a swift kick, I knocked Rizvi to the ground. I raised my fist and was ready to deliver the final blow.

"You should have known better," I said, and added, "You can't defeat me today, and your death is certain. So, tell me, where is Bakari?"

As he fell to the ground, he burst into laughter. Taunting me, he said, "He is your dad! If you dare to be brave, go and find him in Muzaffarabad. By now, he must have learned of your actions here. He will seek revenge for my death by inflicting unimaginable suffering upon both you and your father, thus tearing you both apart. Furthermore, he plans to take your sister-in-law, Sonali, as his mistress, and subject her children to a life of slavery."

Out of anger, I fired at him indiscriminately, even though he was already dead.

I found myself standing amidst the lifeless bodies of my victims, aware that I had little time left. With nimble movements, I expertly planted bombs on each floor of the building. As I descended towards the ground floor, I caught a glimpse of the CCTV room and did not waste a moment before breaking in. I quickly located the recording hard disk and removed it from the system, erasing any trace of my presence. To ensure that I would not be monitored any further, I meticulously disconnected all the Wi-Fi cameras, thus severing their connections with precision. Satisfied with my work, I made my way out of the room, confident that my actions had secured my safety and eliminated any possibility of incrimination.

I stepped out of the building, and with the press of a button, the entire building erupted in a series of deafening explosions with flames leaping up to the sky.

As I tried to process the chaos around me, my phone buzzed with a message from an unknown sender. "Leave the city immediately. Use the waterway, and you will be supported," it read.

But I just could not leave without seeing my father one last time. Wrapping a scarf around my face, I approached the home. As I drew closer, my heart sighed with relief. Dad was playing with the kids. Delighted, I did not want to disturb him and probably wanted to return with a smiling and happy image of him, knowing that I would be seeing him for the last time. Even from a distance, I could see the love and kindness in his eyes, and I knew I would miss him dearly.

I could not stay and returned—the chaos of the city was escalating by the minute. Police sirens blared and the streets were crowded with panicked people. I knew that it was time to leave.

I went to the riverbank, where the same priest who had helped me before was waiting with a boat. "You must leave now," he said firmly, with his eyes filled with concern.

As he began to row us away from the city, I whispered, "Lord Shiva," as my heart felt heavy with grief.

"Please watch over my father, Sonali and the children. Keep them safe and bring them peace," I prayed.

With a heavy heart, I watched the city disappear into the distance.

Chapter 4

The Transit – On the Go!

"Avinash, I'm running late for work. Can you quickly get ready and prepare breakfast for Aditya? Don't forget to pack your lunch. I'll see you in the evening," Aditi instructed.

I embraced her tightly, giving her a warm hug and kissing her forehead before she left. Her eyes sparkled with affection as she looked at me, and she replied, "I love you!"

I woke up from a bittersweet dream, feeling a pang of sadness and nostalgia. As I stretched and got out of bed, my phone rang. It was a missed call from Jagdeep Uncle—a reminder that nothing was left but cherished memories.

Lost in my thoughts, I heard a soft knock on my door. I cautiously opened it to find Jagdeep Uncle standing there, tightly clutching an old laptop.

"Why didn't you tell me you were back?" he whispered and quietly entered the room. "Riyaz called me and informed me that you were here. We must meet him tonight at 11 p.m. sharp. He will send someone to pick us up. But before that, we need to accomplish two tasks."

Feeling curious, I asked him what those tasks were.

As I pondered about the second task, Jagdeep Uncle suggested that we should reach out to my college friend,

Suresh, who could be trustworthy and skilled in IT. However, when I inquired about our next plan, he informed me that Riyaz had not provided any further details yet. Jagdeep Uncle then handed me the laptop and said that he would leave, and planned to meet me again in the evening.

As the day drew to a close, I spent my final moments in the house that Aditi and I had lovingly purchased—to build a life together. It was a bittersweet farewell to my birthplace, the city of Banaras, and now, this home. With nothing more than a family photograph and a few clothes to my name, I donated Aditi and Aditya's clothing to a local NGO, hoping that they would provide warmth and comfort to someone in need.

While I was lost in my thoughts, my phone suddenly rang, thus breaking the silence of the empty house. It was my father on the other end of the line, and I eagerly answered the call.

"Hello, Dad!" I exclaimed, feeling grateful for the distraction.

"How are you, my son?" he asked.

His voice sounded shaky, and it had been a long time since I had heard from him. A sense of peace washed over me, just from hearing his voice but before I could respond, he spoke again.

"Thank you very much for everything," he said. "The deaths of Rizvi and Bhairav have brought us a lot of relief and peace. It's an end to the continuous harassment that Sonali and the kids had endured, and it's an end to the abuse that I suffered. Now, I can sit at the door comfortably, waiting patiently for you to come home."

His words hit me hard. I had no idea their situation had been so dire. I felt grateful that things had improved for them, but I also felt guilty for not being there for them sooner.

"I wish I could see you before you leave from here," Father said—his voice was filled with emotion.

"I wish the same, Dad," I replied. My voice was trembling. Immediately, I burst into tears and sobbed loudly.

Trying to regain my composure, I was met with deep silence on the other end of the line. "Are you there, Dad?" I asked.

"Yes, I'm here, and wondering what makes you so weak, still," Father replied. "It's a matter of pride and honour for me that you did something for us, which we saw as never-ending torture. You have punished two people who took everything from us. There's no need to cry or be sad. You couldn't have done anything better for me, Sonali, and Prakash's kids. I am proud of you. You have fulfilled all your responsibilities towards your father, brother and family members. It's time for you to find peace now."

"Listen, Avinash. I know that I have always been biased about you," Father continued. "I always gave more preference to Prakash. Your mother would often say that I was being unjust to you. I want to say sorry to you today and admit proudly that you have been a great son—for always taking care of all of us. You are like your mother—a fighter who never gives up. I am saddened to see you in this state but you must finish what you have started."

Then his phone beeped, promptly indicating that a message had come in. He checked it and surprisingly asked, "Why have you transferred so much money into my account?"

"This is for you, Dad," I replied. "Please take good care of yourself and everyone else. We might not be able to meet or speak frequently but I will ensure your well-being as long as I am alive," I reassured him.

Father remained quiet for a while before I spoke again. "Dad, you have made me the strongest person alive. I was clueless, disappointed, helpless and hopeless. You gave me a purpose and the strength to stand up for my justice."

"Just do one last thing for me," he said and continued, "Speak to your father when you know it's the right time."

The phone got disconnected, and I remained seated in the room, staring blankly at the wall, lost deep in thought about everything that had happened in the past few months.

As I sat there, memories of the house flooded my mind—of precious moments spent with Aditi, and the fun hide-and-seek games played with Aditya. My eyes roamed around, inspecting every corner of the house as if they were searching for traces of them. The house still held the warmth of Aditi and Aditya's infectious laughter. It felt as though they were watching me from some hidden place, playfully eluding my sight.

The phone beeped, and I received a message that read,

Dinner is ready as per the scheduled time. Hope to see you. Follow your navigation. "

I immediately received a map. Knowing it could not be anyone other than Riyaz, I left immediately. On the go, I continued receiving multiple locations, one after another.

An old factory looked like it had been closed for many years. I entered and kept moving until I reached a dark room. It was only a few seconds after I entered. The room glowed with big screens across the walls that were playing the video recording of what I did in Banaras with Rizvi and Bhairav. Before I could react, someone attacked me from behind with a powerful kick on my back. Controlling myself, I took a few steps forward. I immediately came into action and reverted an even stronger one at him thus making him fall to the ground. It was not over but just the beginning. Five people began to attack. There was no time to think about why and who, so I responded quickly, aggressively and powerfully, knocking them down with multiple punches in the face and kicks.

"If you had lost today, I would have shot you."

The screen was off, and the lights in the room were on. I looked up and saw Riyaz and Jagdeep standing in front of me. "Impressive," he said.

"Who are they? Why did they attack me? And what is this for?" I asked aggressively.

"Oh, so many questions. I wish I could ask your enemies to send you a formal invitation before attacking you," Riyaz replied in a teasing voice.

"I didn't mean that," I said softly.

"What you have embarked upon and stepped into is a one-way road where only two options exist. Either you kill or you get killed. After the Banaras episode, you have gained notoriety and are now under terrorist groups' and agencies' as well as Indian police's and intelligence's scrutiny. They are actively searching for you, the one who has caused a sudden and impactful disruption. They recognize your face and are sparing no effort to gather any and all information about you, all with the ultimate goal of reaching you. Their purposes and perspectives may differ, but their objective is singular—to apprehend or eliminate you. Consequently, my dear, you will find yourself in the dark about many aspects, such as why and who, from this point forward," Riyaz cautioned.

"For your curiosity, these are my people as I wanted to clear my doubt if you have become overconfident," he spoke.

"So, what did you find," I asked.

He approached me, and handing over a big yellow envelope, replied, "Let your questions give you the answers at the right time."

Handing over a yellow envelope, he said, "This is you from now onwards."

Without asking another question, I patently opened it. It had a passport, the holy book, the *Quran*, and a good amount of Pakistani rupees.

It was an Indian passport. It had my picture on it but was named *Shahid Khan* from Kashmir. I looked at him in surprise.

"I understand that you are in a confused and unsettled situation, Avinash. Perhaps, there is one last thing that I realized now which is important to teach you—understanding and learning *Islam* and its culture. This is important, and you need to be there, one amongst them, so that they accept and trust you," Riyaz said.

I placed the *Quran* on my forehead and asked, "Is it not wrong to do all this under the guise of religion?"

"Religion? True religion teaches us to help the weak, spread love and create a peaceful and harmonious world for everyone, regardless of their beliefs or background. The actions of individuals like Murtaza Arzai, who exploit religion for their gain are not acceptable and are against the very essence of Islam. It is important to understand that Islam means peace, and the teachings of the *Quran* emphasize love, compassion and unity.

I am glad that you have the opportunity to seek blessings from Allah and are getting a chance to understand and learn this holy religion. Believe me, if you religiously follow the real meaning of this religion, no one can stop you from reaching your goal. It's important for your mission," he said.

He signalled his people to leave and asked me to quickly come back after properly washing his face, hands and feet. I did as I was asked to do.

He began to teach me about the Islamic religion, its true meaning, values, rituals, culture, the way to worship God, dressing and everything which was required of me to become *Shahid Khan* from *Avinash*.

"Never look at the religion of a person but only focus on humanity. You do not know whom you will encounter. Always strive to discern between what is right and wrong. Do not forget to help what is right and punish what is wrong. May God always protect you," Riyaz said in a heavy voice.

His eyes were moist.

As I touched his feet, I felt a sense of reverence and gratitude for the man who had transformed me. "Thank you for all that you have done for me. I could never have become this person without your guidance and support," I said.

He looked at me with a sense of pride and affection. "You have a long way to go, my child. I will always be worried for you."

"What is my further instruction?" I asked in a firm and loud voice.

He handed me my next mission—to locate Mohammad Ilyas Bakari before the FKM could reach him. However, it was not merely about eliminating him—it involved gaining the trust of the FKM Chief to gain proximity to Murtaza Arzai, the infamous terrorist mastermind.

To achieve this objective, he instructed me to ask my friend to create a fabricated profile of myself, posing as a devoted FKM follower and terrorist activist. This false identity was to be promoted across different terrorist organizations' networks and websites. It was essential for this profile to be secure and untraceable, ensuring that my real identity remained hidden.

"You are a hero to them, especially to FKM, after killing Bakari's brother and chasing him. Your next destination should be Muzaffarabad. I have learned that Bakari is preparing for his elder daughter, Ruksar's wedding next month. Sana Ilyas Bakari, his daughter, might be the key to gaining direct access to Bakari," he said, a smile on his face.

"This may be our last meeting, and I truly hope to see you alive after you bring Murtaza to his fate. All the agents and undercover officers of India are aware of your existence, and out of respect for me, they will not interfere with your work. They cannot provide you with direct or indirect support but they will do their best to keep you out of trouble. You will be completely on your own there, so remain vigilant, cautious, calculative and smart enough to handle any situation," he added.

Lastly, he warned me about Vijay Chauhan, ACP, one of the most astute and intelligent officers of the Indian National Intelligence Agency. I had to stay two steps ahead of him because he had a vast network and detested failure. If he managed to uncover my true identity, Shahid's life would be in grave danger.

As I was about to depart, Riyaz spoke, "Avinash, there was someone who aided Murtaza Arzai in safely escaping—on the night of the hotel attack. It was the hotel's security head, Rajinder Sodhi. I shared this information with the intelligence but they prefer to maintain the belief that they captured the terrorist Mohammad Kamaal Hisab, and the rest were eliminated. Nevertheless, I trust that you know what needs to be done with him. I am certain he has valuable information that can aid our cause."

Handing me an envelope, he continued, "Sodhi is currently in Delhi. He must have received a significant sum of money and is involved in the export of dates and dry fruits. You will find his details enclosed in this envelope. Meet him before proceeding to Muzaffarabad. I'm sure he'll be pleased to meet you as well. Now, you can go," he concluded.

I nodded in acknowledgement and took my leave.

Suresh did as was suggested by Riyaz. A highly encrypted message about Shahid Khan (my new identity) was being sent. All the terrorist agencies were on alert and looking for my next action.

"I can't thank you enough for helping me, Suresh. You knew the dangers involved, but you still agreed to support me," I expressed my gratitude.

"I understand what you're going through. Your decision to take on this task is beyond what most people can even imagine. I stand by you today and always. Don't hesitate to ask for anything you need. Your friend is too clever to be caught by anyone, and you know I'm the best at what I do," he said, smiling warmly and embracing me tightly.

"Wherever you are in this world, whenever you need my assistance, just send me this image using any means—email, message or even post it on the internet—and I'll know you need me. Your friend will reach you without delay," he said, holding my hand firmly.

"Please don't spare that despicable person. None of them should meet an easy death," he added, smiling.

"Goodbye, my friend," I bid farewell, and with that, I left.

Chapter 5

Muzaffarabad

Delhi, June 2009.

Sana Ilyas, the younger daughter of Bakari, possessed undeniable beauty with striking features that could easily turn heads. However, her impressive qualities extended far beyond her looks. She was a brilliant scholar of psychology, who boasted that she had a razor-sharp mind and an exceptional understanding of human behaviour.

Nevertheless, her intelligence and beauty were often overshadowed by her rude and arrogant demeanour. Sana was not one to be easily fooled and tended to treat people with disdain. She did not believe in sugar-coating her words or engaging in polite conversation. Her arrogance was evident in the way she looked down upon those whom she considered beneath her. Her privileged status and wealth only served to amplify her sense of superiority over others.

Despite her many admirable qualities, Sana's rudeness and arrogance made it challenging for people to warm up to her. Her lack of social grace and tendency to belittle others made her a difficult person to be around. While she may have been a gifted scholar, her interpersonal skills left much to be desired.

At that time, Sana was busy shopping for her sister's wedding in Delhi, armed with a long list of items. Thanks to the assistance of Suresh, I obtained all the necessary details about her within a short span of 48 hours. I was well-informed about her daily schedule, shopping preferences and preferred shops as well as brands. The wedding was scheduled for June 21st in Kashmir, and she was in a hurry to complete her shopping, just as I was in a hurry to fulfil my mission.

I somehow managed to secure a job at Rajender Sodhi's wholesale shop within just a week. Strangely enough, I quickly became his favourite employee. However, things took a difficult turn when I discovered that Rajender was gay and had developed a strong attraction towards me—specifically my muscular physique. He began making inappropriate advances, including unwelcome touching, making suggestive jokes and trying to keep me at the shop for longer than necessary.

I genuinely struggled with the situation, feeling uncomfortable and unsure of how to handle Rajender's unwanted attention. To complicate matters further, the other workers at the shop grew jealous of Sana's preferred status and higher pay.

While I contemplated the easiest way to deal with Rajender, which was to end his life, I knew that it was not yet time for that. I had to wait a few more days. I was eagerly anticipating Sana's arrival, as she had to pick up a thousand dry fruit packets as gifts for the wedding guests. Rajender's shop was known for its premium variety, making it the ideal place for her to visit.

Finally, the day arrived, and Sana made her grand entrance into the shop by commanding attention with her presence. Dressed in a pristine white ensemble, her jet-black goggles added an air of mystery to her appearance.

Her long hair cascaded down her cheeks, added to her regal demeanour. She exuded the aura of a princess, accompanied by her retinue of loyal attendants.

As she entered, one of her attendants quickly cleaned a chair and offered it to her. Sana settled into the chair with poise and surveyed her surroundings with a discerning eye. After a brief observation, she turned to one of the employees and inquired, "Who is the owner of this shop?"

The employee humbly replied, "Please tell me how I can help you, Ma'am."

Sana responded with a rude tone, "I don't think you listened to me carefully. I asked who the owner of this shop is, and clearly, you are not the one. Nor do you have the authority to do as I say, I presume."

The employee replied with a smile, "Certainly, Ma'am but I will do my best to meet your expectations. If you could please let me know what you desire."

"I am here to shop. Would you mind asking the other customers to immediately vacate the shop? I need a thousand gift packs of dry fruits and mind you, I want the bigger ones," she demanded with authority.

The thought of providing a thousand gift boxes was overwhelming for Sodhi, and he was taken aback. Seizing the opportunity to introduce myself to Sana, I gently placed my hand on Sodhi's shoulder and requested, "Please allow me to handle this customer, Sir."

I could see an electrifying effect in Sodhi's eyes from my gentle touch. I approached Sana and said, "I am here to assist you. Please let me know your requirements."

She lowered her goggles slightly and replied, "So, you are the owner?"

Before I could respond, Sodhi interjected in a loud voice, "He is my best manager, Madam, and I'm Sodhi, the proprietor, at your service."

Sana remained unimpressed and remarked, "Still, you look better and more sensible than all the other employees. What is your name? And would you mind asking all the customers to leave while I am here?" she ordered him.

"My name is Shahid, Madam, and I don't see any need in asking any of my esteemed customers to leave because you are here. Please enjoy our hospitality and feel conformable. Allow me to show you all the options to meet your requirement," I replied, signalling one of the staff to offer her water.

"Certainly, you don't know who I am, and you should have been careful before replying to me in such a rude matter. Forget about shopping here and listening to your nonsense—I would prefer leaving and why shouldn't you be thrown out for this insolence and disobedience of yours?" she replied aggressively, asking her bodyguards to do the needful while moving out of the shop.

I quickly caught hold of her hand and requested apologies for the impudence.

"It does not suit a big personality and a beautiful woman like you to get so angry. Why do you want everyone to leave? Let them see your royalty, elite class and richness," I said politely.

But her bodyguard did not find me to be polite anymore. Threatening me one of them said, "How dare you hold her hand!"

I stared at him and said, "Leave it, Sir, please act wisely. There'll be a wedding in the house. Why do you want to put Madam and yourself in trouble? Delhi is far away. You can't harm me till Kashmir," I whispered with a cunning smile.

Surprisingly, there was no anger on Sana's face but a smile. "We'll do our shopping from here, Atif," she said giving orders, and she came inside and sat on the chair.

"Now will you keep looking at me or will you show me something?" she replied with an attitude.

As I began to show her options, she kept looking at me carefully without a blink of an eye.

"This is the best we have, and I think it an ideal return gift for the guests, *Dear Princess*," I said, smiling and looking deep into her eyes.

"Then why waste any more time?" she replied.

"It's a deal. I want 1000 boxes of this. How soon will you be able to deliver them?" she added.

Interrupting her, and jumping in between, Sodhi said, "At least a week."

"That's not possible. The marriage is in four days. I need it in the next two days only and I am sure your manager is smart enough to do so. Isn't it, *Shahid?*" she said in a flirtatious tone.

Being a big and expensive order, Sodhi never wanted to miss out on such an opportunity to earn a good amount of money. He agreed.

Sana made the full payment in advance, and as she began to leave, she said, "Well, I forget to mention one important thing. Send the order with Shahid well before time. And if it doesn't go as I say, I know very well how to take my money back."

Maybe this was my chance. I also replied bluntly by saying, "Yes, of course, *Princess,* as you say. After all, I will also get an opportunity to visit my hometown in Kashmir on this pretext."

"Oh, so you are from Kashmir in India? I am from Kashmir in Pakistan. Never mind, the wedding is in your Kashmir. I'll be waiting for you," she said.

I looked into her eyes and said, "Kashmir is the only state which belongs to us and only us. Let India claim it. We have taken half of it already and the day is not far to *own it completely*. Am I right, *dear Princess?*" I asked.

"As soon as you reach Jammu, inform us, and I will make arrangements for your travel further. Atif, give him your number and be nice to him," she ordered.

"You are an interesting man. Nice to meet you. I am overwhelmed by this name— *Princess*," she said, giggled and turned away.

She looked back several times and I also kept looking at her.

Sodhi made workers work day and night and the order was complete. He was very happy. Sodhi's biggest weakness was his greed for money—he could do anything to get it.

The next day, I had to leave, and on the same night, he invited me to his house. As I had no option, I reached his house. He was alone and drinking.

"Do you live alone, Sir? Where is your family?" I humbly asked.

"Why? Do you want to have a honeymoon with my wife? Stupid boy," he replied in anger.

"Stay in your business, and don't ask unnecessary questions. Sit down, have a drink and enjoy the evening. We have closed such a wonderful deal and all credit goes to you," he spoke.

"Why are you sitting so far away? Come close to me. Feel comfortable. I will not rape you," he said and he began to laugh loudly.

He was intoxicated and started touching me strangely. I felt like breaking his hands and putting them in his mouth. But there were still a few moments left in his life.

He began to rub his leg along with mine. "You like me, right?" I asked smiling at him.

He looked at me, took a deep breath and replied, "Undoubtedly!"

"You are a smart hunk, tough and deadly. How will I live without you for so many days? But what am I to do—I am helpless. I wish I could send someone else. Such a big order, so much money and that arrogant woman," he said irritably.

Coming close to me he said, "I am thinking, why don't we spend the night together and make it a memorable one?" he said in a cheesy voice.

It was becoming very difficult to bear the situation by then. Riyaz said that he would have some important information for me, which gave him a little more grace time to be still alive. Smiling, I offered him a drink. He thought he had won the lottery. "I guess, you like me too, naughty?" he said.

"Yes, you are such a hardworking, intelligent and shrewd businessman…so rich and classy—can I become like you? I can do anything for it—as much hard work as is required," I said putting my hand on his shoulder.

Laughing out loud and clapping, he said, "Hard work is for the poor people. Wise ones like me, create opportunities, grab them, get benefits and live a luxurious life. I was never as rich as I am today. I am a perfect blend of smartness and intelligence. Not many are like that," he said in a proud tone while settling on the sofa.

"I want to make you my mentor. Please guide me on how I can be just like you. How did you become so rich?" I asked.

Whispering in my ears, he said, "*Contacts—high profile friends*. I was never so rich until the last few months. I was only earning a few thousands while working as the security-in-charge in a premium hotel in Mumbai and living a below-average life. One day, a very rich man came from Dubai to the hotel."

I quickly grabbed his hand and asked in excitement, "Which hotel?"

"Oh, don't disturb me and listen carefully. Have you heard of the Hotel Taj where there was a terrorist attack recently?"

I nodded and he continued.

"It's the same hotel. It's one of the most expensive hotels in India and he booked half of it for a week. He was from some royal family, and I was assigned to ensure the security of all of them. One day, he called me to his room. I had never seen a suite until that day—so huge and beautiful."

"Such a big man but so humble—he made me sit next to him and offered to have dinner with me. We talked."

"'I want to make a similar and a much bigger hotel than that in Dubai. Would you mind showing me every corner of this hotel so that I can have the best masterpiece designed?' he spoke."

"Hesitatingly, I replied, 'Sir, we are not allowed to do so, and we do have limited access to this hotel. You are a great man who has been so kind and treated a small man like me so wonderfully well. I am genuinely sorry for not being able to help you but certainly, I can speak to my manager about it. You are one of our most prestigious guests and surely, he would help you.'"

"'I am not a great man. I simply understand the true value of people, their time and ensure the best reward for their efforts. I thought you have the desire to do something big in life but you look like someone who likes to offer charity to others—like you just wished to offer this wonderful opportunity to your manager and miss out on your own—a chance of earning a few crores in return. Never mind, I will speak to him directly. You may leave after finishing your dinner,' he said."

"As soon as I heard that, my eyes widened, and I felt a lump in my throat. I didn't know how many zeros were in a crore, and he was offering me that sum. 'But how will I manage the security cameras?' I asked."

"He kept a mid-sized bag before me and said, 'This will be your solution.'"

"With trembling hands, I had just opened the bag, and my breath got stuck. There were countless bundles of 1000 rupees notes and 15 to 20 gold bars."

"'It can all be yours. The condition is that this matter should remain only between us. If you do good work, you will get more rewards,' he spoke."

"I thoroughly showed him the entire hotel. He was very happy with me. He often used to visit the hotel for information on the design work. We became great friends. Every time he came, he gave me expensive gifts and money. Because of him, my life had changed. I came out of poverty and started living a good life. He owed me a lot, and one day, I also got to repay his favour. Terrorists attacked the hotel. He called me in panic and said, 'My brother and one of his friends have been caught in the attack. Both are very dear to me. Either way, get them both out of the hotel safely. I will do you a great favour. In return, I will give you two crore rupees.' he said pleadingly."

"I got them both out safely. And do you know, later, I came to know that both were also *terrorists*? But that's fine—this was out of friendship—and money," Sodhi said in a muffled voice.

"Don't you think many innocent people died because of your greed? Two dreaded terrorists managed to escape because of you," I said.

"Oh dear, no lecture on ethics, please. If I didn't do that, someone else would have done it. And as far as the death of those innocent people is concerned, thousands of people die every day in this world. If I hadn't done it, someone else must have helped them reach a safe exit. Those people were destined to die, if not at that hotel, somewhere else. It's business, my friend, a simple trade. It's the trade of goods and commodities and people too. In the end, what matters is how much money we make. Why are you being so concerned and emotional—as if someone you knew died in that hotel? Just relax, you're with me. Do what I do—fulfil my desire and I will see to it that you are rich too. Don't spoil the mood now. I am feeling sleepy. Let's have some fun on the bed," Sodhi said taking his shirt off.

At that moment, it was difficult to bear him. His words and laughter repulsed me. Aditya's scared face appeared in front of me once again. His painful screams, his begging for his life echoed in my ears.

Showing a picture on my phone, I asked Sodhi, "Was this also the one you helped escape from the hotel that day?"

"How do you know him? How did you get this picture? Who are you? Oh, you are a policeman! Aren't you?" he asked nervously and took out a pistol hidden under his mattress and aimed it at me.

I grabbed his wrist and twisted it until it broke. He was moaning in pain. Pushing him onto the bed, I sat on his chest and shoved the liquor bottle into his mouth, and continued to punch it until the bottle entered his throat.

Blood gushed from his mouth and throat but he was still alive.

"You were right, Sodhi," I said. "Everyone must die one day. But people like you will not decide, when and how. All those people could have lived longer, happily with their families and could have led a good life. It was murder, not your so-called *trade*. You can't even imagine how many lives have been ruined by the madness of some people and the greed of people like you—how many families have been destroyed. I am one of them. The man whom you offered an easy escape killed many innocent people, including my son and my wife. Like me, the loved ones of many more people must have been killed. The burden of their dead bodies is on you too, and you must pay for it now. I am not a policeman but just a *Father, who has decided to take revenge!*"

"You are undoubtedly facing death, and if you happen to be inclined towards an easier way out, would you mind enlightening me on whether the person in this photograph on my mobile is Murtaza Arzai?" I inquired, displaying the image to him.

Tears were streaming from his eyes, suggesting that perhaps, he felt remorseful. I gently removed the bottle from his mouth, allowing him a chance to speak but he remained unable to communicate. With folded hands and a nod of his head, he indicated a positive response by pointing towards his phone. Before I could inquire further, he passed away.

Taking hold of his phone, I extracted the SIM card and destroyed it—to prevent any tracking. I also disabled the location services to avoid leaving any digital traces. Prior to departing, I did my best to clean up the surroundings, as well as collect empty bottles and used glasses in a garbage bag. I then went to the washroom to clean myself and recollected a lesson that Riyaz had taught me during our training sessions about using water to eliminate evidence.

I carefully lifted Sodhi's lifeless body and placed it in the bathtub. I filled it with water and ensured that the taps were left open. It was already midnight, and with the utmost caution, I hurried towards the warehouse. The order was prepared and loaded into a mini truck, and I set off for Jammu.

After an uninterrupted drive of over 14 hours, without a single stop, I finally arrived in Jammu as per Sana's instructions. Upon reaching, I informed Atif about my presence, and he had some time to join me. Feeling famished, I decided to grab a meal at a nearby restaurant. As I sat down, I noticed news of Sodhi's murder being broadcast on a news channel. It was during this report that I first saw Vijay Chauhan, whom the reporter questioned about the unsafe environment in Delhi and the shocking killings of innocent individuals, such as Sodhi— particularly in affluent areas.

Vijay Chauhan stated, "No city is safe for an honourable and ordinary person. We are investigating the matter. This is a tragic incident. We have leads and evidence, and we will soon apprehend the culprit. It seems that the victim had many illegal connections and matters, which could also be a motive for his murder. I suspect this might be linked to the Varanasi incident a few months back."

I listened attentively to his statement without batting an eye. Suddenly, someone placed a hand on my shoulder and asked, "Shall we leave, Shahid?"

It was Atif.

"How did you know I was here?" I inquired.

He smiled and replied, "It's getting late. Let's go."

Atif's associates transferred the gift boxes into six or seven different cars, and we headed for Kashmir. I sat in

Atif's car while he drove. He kept glancing at me through the rear-view mirror but I chose to ignore him.

"Was your drive tiring after such continuous driving? How did Sodhi die? Do you have anything to do with it? By the way, you're very cunning and can be devious—you're capable of anything. I don't know what charm you've cast on Sana. Anyway, everything will be revealed soon, and I'll take full care of you," he said sarcastically.

We reached Gulmarg and passed through winding roads along thin mountains, isolated areas and numerous villages. As it was a wedding celebration, the atmosphere was filled with excitement, music, numerous guests and the aroma of delectable food. I kept a close eye on the grand mansion.

"Are you planning something here as well?" Atif asked, playfully nudging me with his shoulder.

"You are not a guest, so, unload the boxes, get them counted properly and as soon as Sana Madam checks, get lost from here," he said.

Why is he inviting his death? Live a little longer, I said to myself. By the way, in my thoughts, I had already done half of his murder.

Pointing to a room, Atif said, "That's your room for as long as you are here. Be a guest for one night, eat, drink and enjoy. Tomorrow morning, as soon as Sana Madam checks the stuff, leave immediately. And yes, till morning, no sneaky business. Don't bother me, even if you need anything," he said and went away with his teeth clenched.

Atif was not my problem. I had to stay there anyhow. It was necessary to meet Bakari as he was the only strong link that could connect me to Murtaza Arzai as soon as possible.

It was freezing cold. After having food, I lay down on the bed and started checking Sodhi's phone. There was a lot of confusing, suspicious, objectional and doubtful content on his phone. There were many short clips of masked women and children shot in a similar pattern and sequence but in different locations. There were lots of messages in special characters and alphabets. On one number, he used to talk often for hours. He was involved in many illegal and wrongful activities. I felt very tired, so I lay down and ended up falling asleep.

I was abruptly awakened by a message from an unfamiliar number. It read, "The hunt for *Shahid* has begun, so, be prudent and strategic."

I deduced that there was someone looking for Shahid and had begun investigating. This message brought me comfort, as I was sure it was from Riyaz. He had been watching over me, as well as safeguarding and guiding me wherever I went.

Riyaz never planned for the best-case scenario. Instead, he emphasized preparing for the worst-case scenario. This principle of reverse planning was ingrained in me—focusing on identifying potential pitfalls and challenges. He had imparted valuable teachings, and one such aspect was the significance of my identity as Shahid. I took great pride in being referred to as Shahid, knowing he was one of Riyaz's finest soldiers.

I still recall the awe-inspiring moment when Riyaz shared the story of Shahid with me. Shahid operated as an undercover agent and lived the life of a terrorist without causing harm to the nation—all while protecting it. He was a master of disguise, and only a select few had seen his true face. Both the Pakistani Army and various terrorist organizations had complete faith in him due to the exceptional work that he accomplished for them, while secretly sharing vital information with his motherland. However, one day, he mysteriously disappeared, leaving everyone puzzled. Unknown to others, Shahid was battling blood cancer, and his health was deteriorating rapidly. He knew that his exposure could lead to severe damage to the nation.

In dire pain, blood would sometimes ooze from his mouth as he coughed, and breathing became a struggle. Finally, one day, he made a heart-wrenching plea to Riyaz by saying, "Release me from the debt of my motherland." With hands folded in supplication, he implored Riyaz to end his suffering.

The burden of protecting his brother and wife, along with the fear of his true identity being exposed, weighed heavily on him during this difficult time. Despite all the sacrifices and loyalty, he now faced an unimaginable dilemma, seeking solace in the hands of Riyaz.

He said, "I am a soldier. You have trained and ordered me to kill the enemy and achieve martyrdom. That's why I cannot take my life. I am a burden to you, my family and my country. Please set me free now."

Riyaz never thought such a day would ever come into his life. Several days passed, but Shahid's condition was getting worse. And one day, there was a sound of a gun firing from Riyaz's room. Sarvnam ran to his room and saw Shahid lying down—dead.

Sarvnam closed his eyes with his trembling hands and covered his dead body with a white sheet. Sarvnam was Shahid's brother. His wife was still serving the nation and was working as a secret agent. She worked as a *maid* at the Pakistan Army Chief's house in Peshawar.

Sarvnam was given the task of creating my identity as *Shahid*. My photograph was replaced on every important document, place and the minutest of possibility which may be cross-checked. And he did it wonderfully well.

That day, when Riyaz told me about Shahid, he said, "He will always be proud that he gave soldiers like him to the nation. You have the responsibility of adding glory to his name and honour."

"I will always do so," I promised myself that day, today and forever.

The next day was important. I slept and waited for the morning. I was asleep when someone knocked on my door. I got up carefully. It was morning already. A woman was standing at the door—probably the house help. She said, "Get ready fast, you are being called. I will come back in some time."

Soon, she left.

I was experiencing some anxiety and tension. Shortly after that, the woman came back and I complied with her request—to accompany her. The mansion was adorned with decorations reminiscent of a wedding. In a spacious courtyard, Sana sat on a throne made of gold, wearing a beautiful silver-white dress, and was focused on writing something. The surroundings were adorned with charming floral arrangements, and a soft breeze made her long hair sway as she continued to write.

"Hello *Princess*," I greeted her.

She glanced my way, acknowledged the gifts and thanked me for the great job that I had done in coming all the way there for the delivery. Although I waited for her to say something more, she continued working in silence.

"I'm glad the gifts pleased you. I must take my leave now, as I have a long journey back," I said, hoping for a response but receiving none.

As I turned to go, I was stopped by a sharp question from her, "Have I given you permission to go? Do you happen to have any patience? Don't you see, I am occupied with work, stupid!" she said smiling.

"Why is it taking so long?" she shouted.

A servant quickly approached, apologizing and offering me a seat. She rudely exclaimed, "Is this how we treat our guests? Leave at once!"

I was handed a wedding invitation with *Shahid* written on it in Urdu.

"When you have come this far, stay for a little more time. Stay till the wedding. I am sure you will love it. Be *your Princess's* guest."

She gestured to a boy and said, "This is the Mukhtar. He will show you to your room and take care of your needs. There is no need to be afraid of him. And yes, Atif will stay away from you. I know he doesn't like you. Now you must rest and get ready for the evening—on time—today is the ring ceremony," she said and went on smiling and blushing.

I had been seeking that opportunity, but something seemed off about Sana's behaviour towards me. She was typically reserved and aloof with others, yet she treated me kindly. I wondered if she had somehow discovered my secret. My mind was flooded with countless questions.

Upon arrival, I was pleasantly surprised to find myself in a luxurious room. As the evening approached, Mukhtar arrived with a large package and informed me that it was sent by Sana Madam. She had requested that I take the initiative for the evening feast. Upon opening the package, I discovered a stunning *Sherwani* inside. After getting ready, I attended the function where I found myself amongst many unfamiliar faces. Suddenly, Sana appeared behind me and whispered, "You look like a true prince—very handsome."

She introduced me to her sister and the groom. Holding my hand, she took me to meet her father, *Mohammad Ilyas Bakari*. He was *the Bakari* for whom I came such a long way.

His eyes were staring at my hand, which Sana was holding. Gently releasing it and smiling back, I extended my hand towards him for a handshake.

"We don't shake hands with elders here. Instead, we bow down to greet them. This is also called etiquette," Bakari said sarcastically. "I think I have seen you somewhere—are you from India?" he questioned.

I replied smiling, "I am from Kashmir, the heaven which only belongs to us."

It was evident that he was not convinced.

"Oh, come on, Dad! You are embarrassing my guest. He is one amongst us, with similar beliefs and thoughts," Sana said interrupting my words.

"Anyhow, enjoy the hospitality. You are, after all, my daughter's guest," Bakari said in a serious tone.

As I left, his eyes kept following me. He whispered something in Atif's ears—I was sure it was for me.

Everyone was in a joyous mood for celebration, eating, drinking and dancing. Sana was with me almost all the time. Many eyes were on me—keeping a tight watch on my every move.

Unexpectedly, I saw someone entering the ceremony area. It was the man who had taken everything from me—the one responsible for my sleepless and sorrowful nights—the one who had laughed while my Aditya begged for his life. Here he was, *Murtaza Arzai*.

I stood amongst the crowd, watching him, a murderer, being welcomed as though he was a saviour. A big smile of honour was on his face. He approached us with his gun-toting bodyguards. As the distance was reducing between us, my anger and hatred swelled. It was time for justice to be served, and I was ready to make him pay for his crimes.

As he drew nearer, Bakari stepped forward to greet him with a hug. "Welcome, Ikhlaq Sahib," he said warmly. I was confused—I knew this man as *Murtaza Arzai*, so why was everyone referring to him as *Ikhlaq*?

Bakari continued, "I thought you might not be able to make it. I'm glad you did."

"After all, we are still friends, aren't we? And congratulations on your daughter's marriage," he replied with a cunning smile.

I kept my eyes fixed on him, trying to read his expression. Sana was also watching him, stealing glances and showing a mixed expression of restlessness and anger. After exchanging gifts with the bride and groom, he and his entourage made their way to a private room. Clearly, tension existed between him and Bakari, though they both tried to hide it with forced smiles.

"Who is he? He looks important," I asked Sana.

But she made an excuse and left, leaving me to watch from a distance. As I peered into the room through the mirrors, I could see them talking, and their expressions growing increasingly serious.

Suddenly, I was interrupted by Atif and a tall bodyguard. "Where are you going?" Atif demanded.

"I was looking for the washroom," I replied, trying to sound innocent.

"This area is private—only for family members. Please leave and go to the washroom on the other side," he said—his tone threatening me.

I left with my head down, still determined to find out more. I searched for Sana, eventually finding her in her room, drinking and crying.

"Can I come in?" I asked.

She looked up at me, her eyes red from tears. "Now you've come. Why bother asking? Just come in and lock the door."

I hesitated for a moment, unsure of how to help her. "Can I do anything for you, Sana?" I asked.

"Stop calling me *Princess*," she said softly, her voice trembling with emotion.

She continued to drink and was sitting on the floor. As I passed by the door and windows, celebratory music approached my ears. Breaking the deep silence, I asked, "Why have you come here, leaving the party, sitting alone, feeling upset and crying?"

She looked at me and asked, "Have you ever seen loved ones killed before your eyes and you couldn't do anything except cry and suffer? What you could only do is, watch helplessly—silently. *I have seen* that—seen my life, my love and my only support—dying and taking his last breath in my arms," she spoke.

"And what is more painful is to see that murderer around you alive, happy and smiling. You asked me who that man is. He is that murderer who killed my husband, *Imtiaz* just because he could not finish one of his tasks."

"Today, he is in front of me again, and is being treated with respect in my own house and I cannot do anything other than hide here and cry."

What should I have told her? I had also seen my wife and son dying in agony. Their murderer was also in front of me that day and whom I would surely kill. I continued listening to her and she kept speaking and sobbing.

"I know you think of me as a proud, arrogant and rude woman, right? But it's not like that, Shahid. I wear this mask to save myself from many people around me who, like vultures, are ready to scratch me as soon as they get a chance. A widow and a traitor's wife are concubines in their society, whom they take away as their right to make them victims of their lust every night. My inner suffocation reigns in me. If anyone in this house is concerned about me and stands as my shield, then it is my father-in-law, Bakari. But he has also become very weak and very helpless," she spoke.

"I always thought you were his daughter," I said.

"Yes, I am. That's what he considers me to be. But I am his daughter-in-law. Imtiaz was his only son who could not become cruel like his other cousins and people in the group. The madness of these people to occupy Kashmir killed my Imtiaz. Do you know what was his mistake? He had spared the lives of two small children."

"Additional Director General of Police (ADGP), Kashmir, Venkat Somani was giving a tough time to all the terrorist activities in the region. His popularity was increasing day by day. There was peace in the valley. People felt safe. He had become everyone's hero, which was unacceptable to them. A plan was made to kill him publicly at *Gulabi Chowk* so that the same panic would be created again in people's minds. This task was assigned to Imtiaz. Coincidentally, Venkat was out with his family that day. Imtiaz and his associates attacked his jeep with a rocket launcher. The scraps of the car flew away. Venkat and his wife were killed but the blast threw his children away. To ensure Venkat's death, they fired at him as well. His wife was still alive. Imtiaz asked his men not to fire at his wife and did not do so himself. He left Venkat's children and wife alive, although she died shortly after due to severe injuries. This was not acceptable to these people—the fact that Imtiaz showed kindness to his children. He said we had enmity with Venkat and not with his family. Imtiaz was declared a traitor, and at the behest of Lashkar's boss, he was publicly hanged upside down and shot with bullets. His dead body kept hanging on the square for hours. We watched helplessly. I don't know how many more will be killed for and in the hope of gaining Kashmir," she spoke.

"Everything has a price. If you want Kashmir, then you will have to pay the price. You are shedding tears while losing your loved one. So many innocent people have been killed here, are being killed, and will be killed. They neither reason nor are at any fault but still they get killed. I don't know who wants this Kashmir, but many have been paying the price and don't know how long," I spoke.

She looked at me carefully, approached me, held my hand, and said, "The day when I first saw you in Delhi, I felt as though I had met Imtiaz. You think and talk just like him. He never understood why, but he had no choice except to, and so he did. He never wanted Kashmir—neither I nor you, I am sure. It is only the longing and ambition of people like Murtaza Arzai who want to establish their kingdom over the dead bodies of people by spreading terror. People like us want to live with love and peace. We want a house in which we can live comfortably. I am tired of this fear and panic-stricken environment. I do not wish that one day, my dead body would be counted amongst several unclaimed dead bodies. I want to live, Shahid, with you. Please take me from here. I love you. I liked you the first time I saw you," she said, holding me tightly.

"Murtaza Arzai, who is he?" I asked.

By now, I understood that Sana knew a lot more about him. It was not right to play with someone's emotions but I had no choice. I gave her the trust and belief that I too, like her.

"Murtaza Arzai is a belief," she stated firmly. "He is the chief of Lashkar who proclaims that our fight to acquire

Kashmir and our existence will persist only as long as we are engaged with India. According to him, we are not committing any wrongdoing. Rather, it is the will of Allah. We are determined to liberate this heavenly land from the clutches of those infidels and establish our place. God has entrusted us with this task. Those we eliminate are considered infidels, and those of us who fall in battle are hailed as martyrs."

"But my Imtiaz was declared a traitor, not a martyr," Sana said, crying.

I asked Sana, "So, the person who came to meet Bakari today is not Murtaza Arzai?"

Sana replied, "Yes, that's correct. He is *Ikhlaq Arzai,* his third brother. There is some crucial security information that Bakari has refused to share since the murder of Imtiaz during his mission in Delhi for the parliament attack."

"They are pressuring Bakari to share the information as they plan something big again in Delhi. It is believed that some CCTV footage and blueprints of Lashkar were kept with Rizvi, who was living in Varanasi but he was killed a few months ago. Bakari requested them to let his daughter's wedding happen peacefully, after which he would travel to Varanasi to try and retrieve the information," Sana explained.

I was surprised to hear about the third brother and asked, "Third brother? Where is Murtaza then?" And how about his other two brothers?" I asked.

Before Sana could answer, I noticed Atif was trying to peek into the room through the glass window. I gestured to Sana to be quiet.

"Your security official is tough. Atif leaves no stone unturned to ensure your safety. He is keeping a constant eye on you," I said.

"Atif is a cunning and treacherous person who keeps an *evil* eye on his brother's widow. He keeps an eye on me so that I don't run away, or so that Ikhlaq may not harm me—because he often threatens Bakari to harm me if he doesn't share the information. There is no value of relations here—only selfishness, profit and lust exist. Here, anyone can go to any extent for their benefit," she said.

"And how far can you go?" I said, looking into her eyes.

"I don't understand," she said.

But I had understood well. I do not know how but everything was getting connected. Sana was a very important link that could easily lead me to Murtaza. And it was time for some planning and action!

The Sana whom I saw for the first time and got to know that day was not weak and helpless. She was brave, intelligent and courageous.

"If I want, I can take you away from here and all this—even Atif cannot stop me. But how far will you run, Sana?" I spoke.

"Forget about everything. A safe and secure life with loved ones is no less than heaven. Throw away every thorn from your life that pricks and injures you every day. Stop running, face your problems and it's high time to finish them," I spoke.

"Finish them! As in?" she asked me and looked at me in surprise.

I came close to her, put my hand on her shoulder, and said, "Atif and Ikhlaq will have to die for Sana's dignity and freedom. And maybe that's how Bakari also remains safe."

Shoving my hand away in anger, she replied, "Have you lost your mind? Even if I have poured my heart out, that doesn't mean you can start speaking nonsense. And, you know what? Even if Ikhlaq gets a scratch, Murtaza will find us even from Hades and will give us a painful death—something that you can't even imagine. If you want to talk nonsense, you can go—leave me to fend for myself."

"Okay, I'm going from here forever," I said. "But I will pray that you don't meet *Imtiaz* in heaven because if he asks you, 'Sana, why didn't you avenge my murder,' you will have no reply for him. That is, if, after death, true lovers meet. I don't want you to be embarrassed by his question."

I began to leave her room. She called out to stop me from leaving by saying, "Has your *Princess* given you permission to go?"

She came towards me and said, "I am very scared, Shahid. Is this possible—whatever you are saying? Can I be free to live my life with you—without any fear?" she asked.

"Do not be afraid. I am with you and just do as I say. You just must make Atif believe that you started liking him too and hate Ikhlaq very much. As for the rest, I am sure Atif will do the needful," I said.

"Please keep in mind that we have only one opportunity to get this right. Even a single mistake could have serious consequences," I spoke with a focused gaze, looking directly into her eyes.

"Well then, people must be looking for you there at the function. Get ready, my beautiful, and join the party. Atif is continuously keeping a watch on us. He kept asking why I was here and said you feared Ikhlaq and was feeling uneasy. I came to console you and make you feel comfortable."

"And can you somehow stop Ikhlaq here for two days till the wedding?" I asked. She nodded *yes*.

"Can I please hug you, Shahid?" she asked.

She gave me a shy hug and expressed her gratitude for giving her hope in life.

I left her room, feeling detached and emotionless. It was not like me to toy with someone's emotions, but I did what was necessary.

"Isn't it too long to be in the washroom?" Atif asked approaching me.

I chose to ignore him but he persisted and stared at me with an intense gaze—as if he could devour me completely.

Sana also came in after a while. Ikhlaq's hospitality was underway. He was still in the same room with Bakari. His car was now parked at the gate, and he was sure to leave in a few minutes. He exited the room and approached his car and was accompanied by Bakari, Atif and his bodyguards. While he was about to get into the car, Sana said, "Thanks for coming. I would have loved it if you had stayed here till the wedding," stopping him. He was not expecting that. He gazed at her and said smiling, "Where were you? I didn't even meet you today."

"I thought Bakari had hidden you somewhere because of his fear for me. Thanks for the invitation but staying here would not be appropriate. But I can't even break the heart of a beautiful woman like you. I will come to the wedding," he said and left, bidding goodbye to her.

Bakari did not like it but did not say anything to Sana.

The party was over, and all the guests had also left. I was going towards my room when someone grabbed my neck from behind me and threw me against the wall. He was Atif.

He was holding my neck tightly and speaking while grinding his teeth. "Why are you inviting your death? Stay away from Sana. Otherwise, I will kill you."

In just a fraction of a second, the situation had changed. Atif was on the ground, and I twisted his hand and held him tightly and one of my legs was on his neck. He was desperately trying to free himself.

"Oh, Come on, Atif, stop joking. Forget about killing me. You can't even touch me. Can we please focus on treating me with respect? I have been nice, but you turned to bullying. This will not be nice for you, my friend! It will only take seconds to break your neck and change your tense from *present* to *past*. However, I don't really wish to do so but what can I do? I am concerned about Sana. After all, she likes you very much," I said, releasing him from my tight grip.

The enemy bows down or listens to us only when he is afraid of us. Atif needed to be shown his worth.

"What nonsense are you talking about? Does Sana like me? A while ago, I saw you flirting with her. Don't try to make a fool out of me," he spoke.

"I don't need to make anything out of you, Atif, because you are a fool. You have always tried to push yourself towards her but never spoke to her as a friend or a partner who could console and calm her. Do you know what she has been going through? Instead of supporting her, you are continuously hurting her. She only expected your help and support, but you are threatening and controlling her. After today's conversation, I realized how much she still expects from you and looks up to you and only you," I spoke.

The anger and pain on his face turned into a smile. "What are you saying? Does Sana like me? Did she tell you so? What help does she need from me?" he asked.

"That is something which probably, you need to find out on your own. I said what I felt like saying after talking to her. I can only say that she is in great pain seeing Ikhlaq being treated with great respect despite being the murderer of her husband. She is the best one to express herself to you, but today, don't be harsh with her. Rather, be polite and concerned," I spoke.

I did my best. The rest of everything was depending on her now. Pretending to be tired and sleepy, I left from there and watched him by hiding behind the wall.

Deep in thought and with a cunning smile, he stood there for a long time, staring towards Sana's room. I was sure, and he did—he stepped towards her room.

Atif stood there for a long time looking towards Sana's room, and then, his steps moved towards Sana's room.

I hurriedly chased after him with my feet pounding over the pavement. The clock had struck midnight. Atif knocked gently on Sana's door. It seemed as though Sana was not caught off guard by Atif's arrival. She may have been anticipating it.

I observed Atif enter the room and secretly watched them through a small skylight. They conversed for an extended period, speaking softly and making it difficult to decipher their words. It appeared that Atif was attempting to persuade and flatter Sana, who was crying with her head resting on his shoulder. Atif attempted to comfort her and eventually began to kiss her. At that point, I decided to leave the area. Sana removed her clothing and beckoned Atif to join her on the bed.

I felt nervous, upset and slightly worried when I reached my room. Initially, I believed I was playing a game, but then, I was uncertain that Sana was playing her own game. The thoughts kept racing through my mind—before I knew it, I fell asleep in my chair. When I woke up, it was already morning.

There was a knock on the door. As I opened it, Atif hugged me tightly. Thanking me, he said, "I can't thank you enough for helping me get closer to Sana," he said delightedly. "I always thought of you as a cunning, selfish and clever person who came here with a hidden purpose," he added.

I felt relieved as I was doubtful about the situation—the plan was on—as was decided.

"We are friends now. I will ask Bakari to keep you in our team. We need trustworthy, intelligent and sharp people like you. He will be happy to have you on the team. I must leave now. Sana has given me lots of work before the wedding. I need to finish it well on time or else she will get upset. I will not let it happen now. See you in the evening," he said and hurriedly left.

A servant arrived with a message from Sana, informing me that breakfast was ready and that Madam had called for it. Upon arrival, I was directed to a nearby room where only the bride, groom and select relatives were present. As I was served food, Sana whispered in my ears, "Eat appropriately, as it is our last night in the house."

Deliberately touching my hand and playfully suggesting that we could get married that same day, Sana left, smiling, and I began eating breakfast, although I noticed her gaze was fixed on me.

After breakfast and stealing glances from her, I came to my room. As I was closing the door, Sana stopped and hurriedly came inside the room. Hugging me tightly, she said, "Why are you ignoring me, Shahid? Are you angry about something?"

"It's nothing like that. It just felt a little awkward to get close to you in front of everyone. And if anyone has any doubts—if Atif sees it, our plan will be ruined," I said.

She laughed and said, "Atif is an idiot, a birdbrain in a vast body. He is trapped in my clutches."

"But can we trust him completely?" I asked.

"Of course. Now he will do what I tell him. Atif and Ikhlaq will go to Jammu after the wedding tomorrow as they have a secret meeting with some Indian officials. On route, he and his people will kill Ikhlaq. Ikhlaq has a speciality. He is always accompanied by an unknown group of bodyguards known only to him. As soon as he is attacked, Atif and his men will be killed by them for sure," she spoke.

I inquired whether Atif was frightened and retreated immediately. However, she replied confidently, "You don't know me well. I know exactly what he desires. Last night, I granted him his wish—my body. And now, he will do anything to possess me. In love and war, everything is fair. I did it for my love—to win this war for my freedom and to be with you."

As I gazed into her eyes, she drew closer and pressed her lips to mine. "Please don't be upset," she whispered, and added, "It was necessary…to do this."

With a tight embrace, she explained that it was the only way to convince him of her interest.

"Time is of the essence," I said and urged her to leave.

"We must keep our distance until Atif and Ikhlaq's plan is complete. I'll follow them tomorrow to ensure no obstacles arise," I added.

With a nod of agreement, she departed from our meeting spot.

The task at hand was more complex than it initially appeared. A single error could spell disaster, and Sana believed that eliminating both targets the next day would finally exact her revenge and help her gain her freedom. However, my instructions from Suresh were to send him an image or message—whenever I required his aid. The moment had arrived, and shortly after sending the message, he contacted me via an untraceable satellite call. I requested that he should arrange a conversation with someone for me the following morning.

Early in the morning, around 4 a.m., I left Bakari's house and went for a walk in the valley. It was not safe to call from there, and Suresh had connected the call.

The voice from the other side asked, "Hello! What is this?" I took a few seconds to pause before replying, "How are you, Mr. Vijay Chauhan, Sir?"

He did not reply instantly and waited for me to say something else. We remained silent for quite some time.

Finally, I spoke up, "Ikhlaq Arzai will have a meeting tomorrow in Jammu, where he is expected to meet a few prominent and influential people. He is already in Kashmir and would follow the road route. Sir, I hope you know who he is?"

The voice on the other side replied rudely, "Disconnect or continue if you have anything else to say."

I tried to reason with him, "I thought you would consider me to be your well-wisher. However, you may like to visit Rizvi's place in Varanasi, and you might get something important about Bakari and Murtaza Arzai as well."

The person on the other side remained silent, and I waited for his reaction. Meanwhile, Suresh sent a message that I must disconnect the call now.

As I was about to end the call, Vijay Chauhan's voice broke through the silence, by saying, "On a highly-secure satellite call with continuous change in frequency and locations, someone claims to be my well-wisher. And on top of that, he is calling me *Sir* from somewhere in POK. Isn't it strange?"

His tone was sceptical but I kept my cool and waited for him to continue.

"The deep-rooted agencies and intelligence still don't have their exact location and have only heard stories about Murtaza Arzai," he continued, his voice becoming more serious. "Today, someone called claiming to have information about them and is sharing it so easily. Whoever you are, you are not as smart as Vijay Chauhan."

He paused before abruptly ending the call.

I could not help but feel a bit disappointed by his response, but I knew I had to keep moving forward. Vijay Chauhan was a valuable player in this game, and I needed him to create the turbulence necessary to take down Murtaza Arzai. Despite his reluctance to accept my help, I was determined to find a way to get him on my side.

I realized that there is only one shortcoming of honest and proud people. They do not want to take help from anyone in any situation. Vijay Chauhan's reluctance to accept my help was a problem in achieving victory. Maybe he did not take me seriously, but it was necessary to have him in this game because he was the only one who could create turbulence in Murtaza Arzai's life. He was one of the few people who knew that many terrorists had a safe exit from the hotel that day after executing a fatal attack. He also believed that Murtaza Arzai was not only a story but also a living person who was the core of many terrorist activities in the nation.

With my fingers crossed, I was hoping for Vijay Chauhan!

As the sun prepared to rise, I found myself wandering through the chilly valleys of Kashmir, lost in deep contemplation about my life and the immense losses I had endured. I questioned whether I had ever truly gained anything meaningful and what the future held for me. Although fear did not grip me, my mind was restless and heavy with sorrow. Life seemed like an unbearable burden, and in my desolation, I had no one to turn to—not my mother, Aditi or Aditya. I even felt disconnected from my self. My spirit had withered long ago, and the thought of ending my life once again resurfaced. I envisioned closing my eyes and letting go, allowing myself to fall from the mountain to bring an end to everything.

In that haunting moment, I heard Aditya's terrified screams and saw his anguished face. The echoes of his cries still reverberated in my ears. Aditi, too, appeared before me, her hands folded in desperate supplication, pleading for me to save her. However, before I could respond, a single bullet pierced her head, silencing her forever. The sound of the gunshot jolted me. I was awake, drenched in sweat. The rising sun's gentle rays caressed my face, offering a semblance of solace and calming my fear.

I heard my mother's soothing voice say, "This is your reality, Avinash. It will always be a part of you, and that's why you are still alive. You must carry on until the end. Aditya's cries and Aditi's tears demand justice, and it is your duty to honour them."

My mother stood beside me, radiating pride and confidence. Her eyes were dry, and I could sense her unwavering belief in me. "You cannot afford to be weak," she reminded me. "The end is drawing near, and you must remain resolute, confident and strong. Never doubt yourself. You are a good person, and you always will be. Sometimes, to vanquish evil, one must be tough. To defeat a cheat, one may need to resort to cunning and to expose a lie, one must be willing to deceive," she spoke, and I listened intently as we gazed at the rising sun.

I could not discern the moment my mother left after patting my head. Love and trust possess great power. They grant us the ability to achieve the seemingly impossible. My heart felt unburdened, and a fierce determination to fight for justice consumed me. My passion filled me with immense courage and unwavering faith. Yes, my goal was within reach, and there was still much to be done. I offered my reverential bow to the sun with folded hands, turned around and made my way back home.

As I stepped into my room, I noticed that the door was open, and Sana was inside. "Where have you been?" she asked me in a doubtful tone.

"This morning, I noticed that you left the house stealthily as if trying to conceal your departure. What's going on? Is there something fishy? I've trusted you, and you know what we plan to do, but it seems you're hiding something from me."

"I told you, we wouldn't meet until…" I began to reply.

"That's not the answer to what I asked," she interrupted me with an angry voice, pushing me against the wall. "You're hiding something. You're a liar. I trust you so much, love you and see myself spending my entire life with you. I'm willing to go to any extent for us."

"Okay, fine. So go and tell Atif that you're making a fool out of him and that we plan to kill him and finish everything and continue to live this miserable life if you don't trust me," I said.

"Do you think it's very simple to kill both? Lots of arrangements, planning and resources need to be made, and I'm the only one doing that. You need to be patient, so, keep yourself cool, remain vigilant and be careful. And I'm asking you to do this for us. I hope you understand."

As she hugged me, she spoke of her dreams of a happy world with me and pleaded that I should never cheat on her. I looked into her eyes and kissed her forehead while reassuring her that we were doing this for us.

With a smile, she said that she needed to go prepare for the wedding and our safe exit the next morning. I asked if Atif had said anything, and she informed me that they would both be leaving for Jammu immediately after the wedding. Ikhlaq would be accompanied by a powerful Indian politician, and Atif informed her that Ikhlaq would be attacked and killed in Chandanwari because of his strong support there.

She forwarded a route map to me which Atif had given to her—which she guessed was their plan. Additionally, Bakari would be leaving for Varanasi that night because Ikhlaq had threatened to cause harm to all of them if he did not receive the secret information upon his return from the Jammu meeting.

Sana left, thus reminding me to come back because she would be waiting for me to run away from there.

I capitalized on a significant news story about *Bakari leaving for Varanasi* to further gain Vijay Chauhan's trust. I sought Suresh's help to ensure that the information reached Vijay.

As the ceremony progressed, guests began to arrive, and the procession made its way to the venue. Amidst the joyful ambience, which was filled with music and dancing, Sana, Atif and I eagerly awaited the arrival of one important person, Ikhlaq Arze, a vital link that connected our different ambitions. However, with each passing moment, our anxiety grew as Ikhlaq had yet to come, even as the wedding ceremony ended. Sana looked at me with concern.

The long-awaited arrival finally happened, and Sana greeted him with a smile. He adjusted his glasses and declared that he always keeps his promises, especially to a beautiful woman like her. He apologized for being late and acknowledged that she must have been waiting eagerly. His gaze revealed his desire as he remarked that since he fulfilled his promise, he deserved something from her in return. After kissing Sana's hand, he proceeded to greet the other guests and congratulate the newlyweds. Atif, who was possessive of Sana, could not help but feel jealous when he saw Ikhlaq kiss her hand.

After the completion of the wedding ceremony, the guests started to depart, including Ikhlaq, who got into a heated argument with Bakari. Fuming with anger, he kicked the chair and made his way towards his car. He shot a glare at Sana and gestured towards Atif, thus signalling him to come along. Without another word, he drove off in his car.

Ikhlaq departed for Jammu with a convoy of four vehicles and bodyguards. Atif and I trailed closely behind. The cars were travelling at a high speed, and causing our hearts to race. We pressed on by navigating the winding and twisting road ahead.

Atif pointed the gun at Ikhlaq and said, "You and your brother's hooliganism will be over now. How dare you touch Sana!"

Atif shot Ikhlaq's hand. Ikhlaq was mourning in pain. Atif's people and Ikhlaq started firing at each other.

And then what I was not expecting happened—Vijay Chauhan came with a heroic entry, and he, along with his cops, opened fire on both.

There was an atmosphere of chaos. "Ikhlaq has to be caught alive. Give me cover fire," Vijay Chauhan instructed.

His people moved towards him.

I could not allow this to happen. Ikhlaq had to stay alive so that I could have easy access to his brother, Murtaza. I planned to stage an attack on Ikhlaq, orchestrated by Atif, and then gain the trust of both Ikhlaq and Murtaza by saving his life. That was why Atif's death had become inevitable.

Ikhlaq always surrounded himself with dangerous shooters and unknown bodyguards to ensure his safety and security. Their presence made it nearly impossible to get close to him and harm him. This was beyond Atif's capability and control, so inviting Vijay Chauhan to the party was crucial, and he did indeed attend.

Upon my arrival, Atif greeted me with excitement, assuming that I had come to assist him. "Great job, Shahid. Thank you for your help," he said and he expressed his gratitude.

Meanwhile, Ikhlaq was pleading for mercy in front of Atif, and Vijay Chauhan was struggling against Ikhlaq's bodyguards and gunmen at a distance.

"Atif, release Ikhlaq. Let him go," I said, pointing a gun towards Atif's head.

"Have you lost your mind? How dare you point a gun at me?" he retorted, shouting at me.

He aimed his gun at me, but I acted swiftly and fired before he could pull the trigger, aiming directly at his head. The bullet pierced through his skull, causing him to collapse to the ground, lifeless. In a hurry, I rushed to Ikhlaq's side and assisted him into the car. His hand was bleeding, and he moaned in pain as I helped him in.

"Is there any safe place where we can go?" I asked Ikhlaq, concerned about our safety.

Moaning in pain, he asked, "Who are you? I have seen you somewhere, and unless you tell me, we can't go anywhere."

"I have saved your life, and taken you out of danger. You could have either been killed or arrested. Is it not enough? Well, you need immediate medical attention, and the choice is yours," I replied to him firmly.

"Who am I? My name has become associated with the label of a *terrorist*. The state was on high alert, with reports of extensive firing in the valley. News channels were broadcasting the escape of two extremists, including a picture of me and another person named Ikhlaq. Consequently, I became a wanted terrorist and was pursued relentlessly by the police. Vijay Chauhan's blockade was implemented throughout the city, making it nearly impossible to escape."

"We don't have much time and there's a police blockade surrounding us. Let me know if you know of any safe place, otherwise, we'll be caught," I told him in a worried tone.

He handed me a phone and instructed me to follow the directions given by the person on the other end of the line. I obeyed a commanding voice that guided me towards a large mansion. Eventually, we arrived safely.

The place seemed to be the residence of an influential individual, perhaps even a well-known politician. Shortly afterwards, a doctor arrived to attend to Ikhlaq but I could not but help notice his persistent gaze towards me. We were served dinner, and later I was instructed to sleep in an adjacent room.

As I consumed each morsel of food, an intoxicating sensation overcame me, and I eventually lost consciousness. When I regained my awareness, my eyes stung, and my body throbbed with pain. Surrounded by blinding lights, I struggled to open my eyes and discovered that I was suspended upside down by a rope. The merciless beatings had left my body covered in bloodstains and bruised patches.

"Finally, you regained consciousness, *Shahid.* We made numerous attempts to rouse you, exhausting our efforts. Now it's time for you to reveal the truth. Who are you? Refusing to comply will result in a forceful revelation, employing iron rods," Ikhlaq bellowed, firmly gripping my hair.

"How is your hand now? Thanks for the hospitality. You have taken excellent care of the one who saved your life," I said, smiling sarcastically.

"What place is this? It looks very different," I asked.

"Oh, so now you need an introduction. Never mind, I must fulfil the wishes of the one who is to die soon. Welcome to Islamabad, my friend! And if your questioning is done, would you care to open your mouth and tell me who the hell you are or should I continue and kill you?" Ikhlaq said angrily.

"If you intended to kill me, why haven't you done so already? The truth is, I saved your life. Atif and Bakari had planned to harm you but I chose the path of Allah and intervened to protect you," I explained.

"Enough of this nonsense! You may think highly of yourself and believe me to be beneath you but don't underestimate me. Tell me your plan, or else..." Ikhlaq countered, his menacing threats still hanging in the air.

"I have been working for Bakari for a considerable time, but his focus shifted entirely towards seeking revenge for his son, disregarding the cause of a free Kashmir. This contradicts our purpose and duty. As a true soldier, I believe in remaining faithful to our mission, and those who impede it must face the consequences. That is why I made the decision to save you," I asserted.

Though I could sense his wavering trust, Ikhlaq decided to give me a chance. He turned me around, thus revealing a sight that left my eyes wide open in shock. Sana, whom I knew, was in his possession. Her mouth was tightly gagged, and her hands and feet were bound.

"Prove your loyalty," Ikhlaq demanded. "Bakari is of no use to me now. The Indian police have apprehended him. However, I seek revenge. I don't want to kill this beautiful woman but I am left with no choice. I am aware of her involvement in this conspiracy. Kill her, and I will guarantee your safe escape from here. Inflict a painful death upon her, and you can secure your own life. Your time starts now!" he said.

With that, Ikhlaq departed with his accomplices.

Untying myself, I landed on the floor—a skill that Rizvi had taught me. I approached Sana, who stared at me with questioning eyes. I quickly untied her hands and legs and removed the tight bandage from her face. She took a deep breath, as she was surely feeling choked until then.

"How do you plan to kill me?" she taunted me before I could respond.

But before I could say anything, she extended a folded and crushed thick paper towards me—a picture of me, Aditi and Aditya. She had found it in my bag.

"That day, when you went after Atif and Ikhlaq, I decided to stay in your room until you returned," she began. "I wanted to enjoy the memories we shared but I discovered the truth. You were nothing but a fake person. I had the chance to escape but I stayed there for four long days, knowing the truth about you. I wanted to see the face of the impostor, the person I loved so much, whose name and character were all lies."

Tears welled up in her eyes, and her voice quivered with pain as she pointed the gun at me. She asked, "What did I do wrong? Why didn't you even try to tell me the truth?"

I approached her, placing the barrel of her gun against my chest, and said, "Finish me."

The reality was that I could neither save her nor kill her. I could not leave her alive because I knew the brutality and cruelty with which Ikhlaq would treat her eventually.

She came closer and pleaded, "We don't have much time. I want to know your truth before I die. Because no matter how many lies you've told me, I know you're not a bad person. There is love, even if it's just a little, in your heart for me."

"My name is Avinash. I am from India, and my identity is that of a father...," I confessed, revealing everything.

"I'm proud of you and grateful to have known and met you. There hasn't been and may never be another person like you, who has chosen to take on what you have. You're very close to accomplishing your goals, so please don't lose strength and make sure to hold them accountable for what they've done to the people, to you and countless innocents. In our dark passion, desires and hatred, we have forgotten the families we've destroyed. We are all responsible for the bloodshed of many innocents, including myself. Who would have thought that an ordinary man, a father, would one day rise to bring justice for his people—to punish us for our sins? My admiration for you goes beyond love. I have immense respect. I have one last request. Please punish all of us without mercy. We deserve it," she said, sobbing.

"And if I may ask one final thing, could you please hug me once?" she pleaded, with her hands joined.

"Now go, Avinash, and please don't look back," she said.

I turned and started walking, hearing three gunshots behind me. She had taken her own life. I did not look back. I *did not* fulfil her *last wish*—I *did not* hug her.

Ikhlaq had told me about a safe exit, but I knew he was lying. As I left, he and his men were waiting for me.

"Kill him," he instructed.

Rizvi shared an insightful perspective about Murtaza Arzai. According to him, Arzai had a specific criterion for those allowed into his inner circle. Firstly, he sought individuals whom he perceived to be stronger than himself as they would enhance his power. Secondly, he looked for people who were intelligent, quick-witted, greedy and cunning—qualities akin to his own—whom he could exploit for his gain. Arzai's *modus operandi* revolved around instilling fear, and anyone capable of spreading anxiety and panic became a valuable asset. He did not spare even his closest associates when it came to playing the game of fear. Many had met their demise under his command, while others were won over through bribery and manipulation— all to ensure unwavering allegiance. Those who dared to challenge him, opposed his orders or became useless were swiftly eliminated. After the Mumbai attack, a considerable number of his followers had met their end.

Rizvi instructed me to convince Murtaza Arzai that I shared his mission and could be a valuable asset to him. Little did I know that Arzai had been closely monitoring my every move, posing as Ikhlaq. My safe passage into Pakistan and continued survival until this point were not mere coincidences. Arzai had been meticulously observing and testing my loyalty and usefulness.

Ikhlaq confronted me, positioned atop his jeep's bonnet and emanated a formidable aura. Around 20 of his followers encircled him, armed with swords, iron rods and menacing knives—awaiting his decisive order to attack.

Rizvi had instilled in me the belief that true warriors never waste time—they swiftly dispatch their enemies with a single decisive blow, thus showcasing the ultimate glory of their power. And that is precisely what I did.

In a blur of speed, I incapacitated some of the assailants with broken necks, while others fell victim to my sword slashes and knife thrusts. Chaos erupted as their lifeless bodies scattered on the ground. With a sword pressed against Ikhlaq's neck, I watched fear fill his eyes.

However, my triumph was short-lived as a commanding voice interrupted, "Stop right there!"

Turning around, I laid eyes on a formidable woman, standing tall at about six feet, donning a red suit. Her long hair, thick mascara and red lipstick gave her a striking appearance.

"You're alive because we allowed you to live. You've survived because you saved Ikhlaq's life. Let him go and step back," she ordered firmly.

Upon hearing her words, Ikhlaq moved towards her, and they embraced in a warm hug—seemingly sharing a deep connection.

"Indeed, you possess remarkable qualities—courage, agility, strength, youthfulness and intelligence. I commend you for all of them. However, it does not imply that Murtaza Arzai would resort to harming his brother."

With a gesture towards his companion, he instructed, "Take him, with care. He's injured and requires proper medical attention. Ensure that he is treated well. Tomorrow, we will reunite at the camp."

With those words, Murtaza Arzai and Ikhlaq departed, leaving me feeling perplexed. I could not fathom how that lady, whose voice had a touch of masculinity, could be Murtaza Arzai. Something seemed suspiciously amiss. My gaze remained fixed on their retreating figures until they vanished from my sight.

Chapter 6

The Camp

Sanghar is one of the large districts in the Sindh province of Pakistan. It has a high population density and a low standard of living—lacking basic amenities. Unfortunately, it has gained notoriety for being a breeding ground for training camps that convert innocent boys and girls into *terrorists*.

During my time in the city, I experienced a strange sense of suffocation. I was provided accommodation in a small room in a tall building. The room had a broken door and a small window covered in dust and cobwebs.

As I examined the room, the man who brought me there assured me that I would move on the next day. In the meantime, he handed me a packet of food. I stood at the window for a while, feeling tired and even the mosquitoes seemed to have grown weary of buzzing in my ears.

After taking my medicine, I lay down and soon fell asleep. When I woke up, it was already morning, and I could hear the *Azan* prayer echoing from the mosque. There was a knock on the door, and through the broken gap, I recognized the man from before.

Handing me a packet, he informed me that we needed to go far off. He had brought clothes for me and assured me that they would fit. While I got ready, he patiently waited in the room, and soon, we set off.

Unknown to me, while I was sleeping peacefully, Murtaza had been investigating my identity. The man who accompanied me took me to the mosque and informed me that Murtaza would meet me there. As I waited, a woman approached me and embraced me in a quick motion. She whispered in my ear, urging me not to react and revealed that she was Shahid's wife. She instructed me to greet and treat her as my wife, as we were being watched. She emphasized the need to act cleverly and discreetly, as any misstep could bring us great trouble. Rizvi had informed her about me.

I understood the situation, and it was a great honour to meet such a courageous woman who remained dedicated to her duties despite the loss of Shahid, a true hero who had sacrificed everything for our nation.

"Two true lovers meeting at such a sacred place— the mosque," Ikhlaq teased with a hint of playfulness. However, amidst the fallen enemies surrounding us, we knew that utmost caution was still required.

"Your reputation had preceded you, but we needed to ensure your authenticity through a thorough investigation. I must commend your unwavering dedication to our cause by risking your life while living in the enemy country for so long. Your relentless efforts have significantly contributed to our success. We must depart now," Ikhlaq stated, emphasizing the importance of not keeping Murtaza Arzai waiting for too long.

"And I am certain that your wife, Ruksar, also needs to return to the Army Chief's house on time, considering the security protocols," he said.

With hope in my voice, I requested, "May I please have a chance to speak to my wife, Ruksar, in person? It has been such a long time since we last met."

He agreed, saying, "Oh, yes, of course. I will be waiting outside. We all need to move out."

With that, he departed. Four of his men had been hiding in the mosque, discreetly observing our surroundings. Upon receiving his signal, they swiftly left the mosque premises.

"Did Rizvi say anything else?" I asked her.

"He conveyed this message—no matter how great a belief, there is still room for doubt," she said and left.

I also left to meet that person I had been desperate to meet for a long. After a few hours' drive, we reached the camp.

As I entered the camp, I saw small children with guns. A few boys and girls were put on ice, naked. Rough physical training was being conducted for a group of people.

We reached a tent. Murtaza Arzai was sitting in a high place, but that day, he was not in a woman's dress. He looked just as I had seen him that night.

He addressed a gathering of people, deliberately corrupting their thoughts and misleading them. He inspired them to engage in the ruthless killing of innocent individuals under the pretext of *Jihad*. Gesturing to me and Ikhlaq, he motioned for us to take a seat.

His words echoed through the room as he proclaimed, "We are the chosen saviours of Islam. It is our sacred duty to defend it at any cost. Taking lives is not a sin. It is a divine commandment from Almighty God. Failure to comply would result in eternal damnation. We should rejoice in the opportunity to fulfil God's purpose. We must show no mercy, and mercilessly punish anyone who stands in the way of Islam. Only then will we be rewarded with heavenly paradise."

He continued to spew venom against India for hours, passionately inspiring everyone around him with the belief that the war would persist until Kashmir was fully under their control, regardless of the mounting death toll or the numerous attacks required to achieve it.

In a chilling announcement, he proclaimed that an even deadlier attack on India was in the works, surpassing even the magnitude of the Mumbai attacks. He encouraged everyone to feel fortunate to be part of this heinous plan. Despite his instruction to break for lunch and resume training, a profound sense of unease settled within me. This person not only callously took the life of my beloved Aditya but also relished mocking his death. Their faces haunted me—the one sitting beside me and the other standing in front of me—both equally detested. The sinister intentions behind their actions loomed ominously, and I could not help but wonder when, where and how their nefarious plans would unfold.

As I stared at him intently, he questioned why I was observing him so closely. Before I could respond, Ikhlaq discreetly whispered and advised me to greet him respectfully to avoid any offence. Reluctantly, I approached him, wearing a forced smile and bending my knee, and I kissed his hand in a gesture of submission. Despite his unworthiness, I had to comply with that request.

"It's a pleasure to meet you. How could I dare to stare? I simply didn't recognize you yesterday when you were disguised as a woman," I cautiously remarked.

With a pompous demeanour, he declared that no one could truly recognize him—not even himself. He believed that he possessed special powers which were bestowed upon him by divine force, thus enabling him to carry out their work. He regarded himself as both male and female, claiming to be a unique creation of the Almighty.

"I am both—a divine creation. I am God!" he said and burst into boisterous laughter.

Murtaza Arzai, an androgyne, embodied traits of obsession, arrogance, insanity, cruelty and corruption. He believed that he had the authority to punish others, considering his actions righteous and his thoughts infallible. His voice grated on my nerves, and his lack of hygiene left me feeling repulsed.

We traversed through the camp, shamelessly tallying and boasting about the attacks, innocent lives being taken and more. He took immense pride in himself and his cohorts, particularly highlighting the Mumbai attack as one of their most successful missions. The terror and fear they inflicted upon the people excited him, and he pledged to continue sowing chaos, proclaiming that India deserved it for supposedly deceiving them over Kashmir.

The camp presented a disturbing spectacle, filled with chilling moments that sent shivers down my spine. People were inebriated, subjected to drugs and injections and confined like animals in cramped, suffocating rooms, devoid of food and water. Pornographic material featuring Indian and Arab actresses was displayed to the boys.

They were enticed with promises that if they executed their missions successfully, they would be rewarded with encounters with beautiful women and marriages to these revered actresses. Girls, on the other hand, were lured with promises of overseas travel, money, jewellery and gadgets. Murtaza proudly referred to them as his brave and loyal soldiers.

However, these individuals were far from brave, loyal or genuinely interested in Murtaza's misguided ambitions. They were unaware of their whereabouts, their purpose and why they were here. They were victims of the corrupt mindset of those who exploited religion for personal gain. Poverty, hunger and unemployment forced many into this predicament, while some were coerced into it. They were people yearning for a better, more peaceful and happy life. None of them desired to take over Kashmir. They were merely seeking opportunities to build a dignified existence. Their helplessness was exploited, reducing them to mere shells of their former selves. Today, they were nothing more than machines being utilized. When their intoxication subsided, they would cry out and attempt to flee. Those who dared to escape were shot and those who resisted were drugged into submission. The girls were repeatedly raped by multiple people. If anyone got pregnant, their foetuses were either aborted or their child was killed before them. Murtaza called it tough training to make them mentally and physically strong.

Another facet of the camp involved those who willingly adhered to the cause. They received training in firearms, bomb-making and technology. This faction resembled a corporate setting, with talented software engineers, technicians, scientists, doctors and influential

Islamic followers from around the world. The common motives driving these individuals seemed to be greed for wealth and lust. Astonishingly, despite their high levels of education, they had all turned a blind eye to humanity.

I spent two months there, relentlessly working to gain Murtaza's trust and maintain proximity to him. Despite numerous attempts, it became evident that killing him within the camp was impossible. It was important to take him out of Pakistan but the question was how?

As suspicions arose amongst others, I had to carefully eliminate them mysterious. Fortunately, Murtaza had begun placing his trust in me. I assisted him effortlessly with various tasks, some of which were crucial. However, it was important for me not to overstay my welcome. I disregarded my own life, but I had to avoid raising any alarms. Murtaza, fearless as ever, was devising new plans. It was evident that something significant was on the horizon, and it was poised to happen soon.

Meanwhile, the situation in India was deteriorating. Vijay Chauhan relentlessly pursued me, since I was known as *Shahid the Terrorist*. Bakari's suicide in police custody, along with his confirmation of my identity as Shahid, further solidified my reputation as a terrorist. I quickly became *the most wanted person*.

I frequently provided Vijay with tips regarding various attacks, some of which were successful and others were not. However, he began taking my warnings seriously and handling them with caution. I also sent him numerous pictures and videos of the camp. Throughout my interactions, I encountered individuals stationed in India, London, Dubai and Afghanistan—all somehow associated with the terrorist network. Amongst them were senior officials and influential leaders of India. Many were apprehended, a few were eliminated and some were under constant tracking and surveillance.

Murtaza became greatly affected and increasingly irritated by these developments. The growing pressure on him weighed heavily, and he struggled to cope with these repercussions.

Vijay Chauhan persistently attempted to inquire about my identity but I evaded his questions by disconnecting the call every time.

One morning, Murtaza's bodyguard approached me, conveying an urgent summons from Murtaza. I wasted no time and promptly made my way to him. Upon entering his room, I found him engaged in prayer, dressed once again in women's clothing. Respectfully, I positioned myself by the room's wall, patiently waiting for him to conclude his devotions. As he finished his prayers, Murtaza's gaze met mine, and I greeted him, acknowledging his call for me.

"You have been here for some time, and your contribution to the cause has been invaluable. Your assistance with various tasks, some of which were beyond my capabilities, has not gone unnoticed. I truly appreciate your hard work, dedication and unwavering loyalty."

"Let me share something personal with you, Shahid. We were once four siblings, born to the same parents. However, our father felt ashamed of my existence as a eunuch and harboured a desire to kill me. In a tragic turn of events, my mother sacrificed her life while trying to protect me, and in response, I had no choice but to take my father's life. Despite his hatred towards me, he trembled with fear and pleaded for his life in his final moments. It makes me wonder, had he feared me earlier, he might still have been alive today."

"We endured profound loneliness from a tender age and were subjected to exploitation and torture. I cannot even begin to count the number of times I was subjected to sexual assault. One fateful day, filled with fear, I found myself sitting outside a mosque. My clothes were tattered, and my body bore numerous injuries. It was during this desperate moment that a man approached me, and covered me with a sheet. For the first time in my life, someone looked at me with genuine sympathy. His name was Mohammad Wasim Murtaza."

"He taught me a profound lesson about graceful living—never anticipate sympathy from this world. If someone does extend empathy and compassion, they are nothing short of divine. Furthermore, he imparted a valuable second lesson— transform your fear into strength, and the world will inevitably submit to you, for there is no mightier force than fear itself. As life carried on, we grew resilient and unyielding. Sadly, I lost two of my beloved brothers in this treacherous game, and the third would likely have met the same fate if it were not for your presence. You are the second person who extended help and treated us with genuine sympathy. Today, I proudly declare you as my brother."

Murtaza embraced me, with teary eyes and spoke with resolve, "Come, we must embark on a crucial mission."

We departed from his home—the destination was unknown to me. He stayed silent, while I glanced at him repeatedly. The perpetrator of numerous innocent lives mourned his brothers that day. The destroyer of countless families deemed his sorrow paramount. I could not discern the truth of his story, yet I felt no sympathy towards him. To me, he remained a criminal and a murderer.

We arrived at a hotel where a group of individuals, including some foreigners and individuals from the Pakistan Army, gathered in a conference hall. A notable figure, Murtaza, stepped forward to welcome a man who seemed significant. Murtaza extended a respectful invitation for him to be seated. The man introduced himself as Hafiz Saif, the chief of Lashkar-e-Azadi. Once everyone was seated, Murtaza insisted that I sit next to him. With all eyes on me, he declared, "This is Shahid, my trusted companion and brother."

The meeting commenced, and Ikhlaq presented a series of pictures on the projector. The audience was confronted with the harrowing image of the Mumbai attack, followed by visuals of the RBI Bank, Statement's House and India Gate.

Hafiz inquired, "Are all preparations complete?" Murtaza swiftly responded, "Yes, Sir." He continued, "India needs to be taught another lesson—one that surpasses the scale of the Mumbai attacks. The agencies have caused significant damage to us and eliminated many important associates. It seems that they have developed a fondness for fireworks, so what could be more fitting than October 17th when Indians will be celebrating Diwali with fireworks? Let us also join in by targeting three prominent buildings in Delhi with bombings. This will be a resounding blow to India, shattering its backbone and setting people back for years to come. Ikhlaq will lead this mission, with Shahid will handle all the necessary support."

"The team will travel to India via Dubai and Germany, using false identities, three days prior to the attack. Upon their arrival in Delhi, our contacts will reach out to them. Taking advantage of the extended holiday period, it will be relatively easy to plant the bombs in the targeted buildings. The day before the attack, preparations will be made at India Gate as well. All the necessary arrangements have been made. We only require your permission to proceed," he explained.

Murtaza added, "There is one more thing, Sir. Vijay Chauhan, an Indian officer, has inflicted significant harm upon us. It is crucial that he also learns a lesson. On the night of the attack, we will ensure the destruction of him and his family as well."

As I sat there, contemplative, I could not help but wonder about the motivations behind their actions. What would be gained from the loss of innocent lives? Vijay Chauhan had to face the wrath of individuals who did not even know him. What would they truly gain from his demise? It became evident to me that this was more than just an act driven by personal vendettas. It resembled a sinister business, involving multiple countries, countless people and well-funded terrorist organizations, all working towards political and global advantages. It was not solely about instilling fear. It was a carefully orchestrated game fuelled by money and power.

Hafiz inquired whether anyone had anything to add before concluding the meeting.

"Why continue to hide and engage in these covert operations?" I questioned aloud. "Why not integrate India with Pakistan through an all-out war? How long must we persist in these petty conflicts?"

The hall fell silent, absorbing my words. After a moment, Hafiz rose from his seat, applauding and embracing me. "I appreciate your intention and courage," he declared. "We need individuals who are as brave, passionate and dedicated as we are."

His endorsement sparked a wave of applause from everyone in recognition of my boldness.

My message seemed to elude many of those who were present, they failed to comprehend the significance of my words. I sought to expose their true nature, urging them to abandon their hidden tactics and instead confront the battle directly. Only then would they truly discover who harboured fear and who possessed strength. It was a bold declaration, challenging their courage, for if they truly possessed it, they would not have relied on covert attacks for an extended period.

As we drove back to the campus, Murtaza expressed his satisfaction and commended me for my thoughts and fervour to fight for the mission. However, that was not my primary concern. I needed to reach out to Vijay Chauhan and alert him about the impending danger.

Later that night, once we arrived, hastily, I made my way to my room. Once again, I sent the image to Suresh, expecting him to contact me promptly. However, this time it did not unfold as expected. I anxiously waited for his call throughout the night, but it never came.

It was the following morning when I sent the image once more, and this time, he called, apologizing repeatedly for the delay. He informed me about the unfortunate passing of his father, which had caused the delay in his response.

The call was connected, and I shared everything with Vijay Chauhan.

"I want to inform you about one more thing," I said.

"Yes, please," he replied.

Informing him I said, "This time, you and your family are also their targets. Someone is keeping a close watch on your movement. Please be safe."

"I don't know who you are, but you are doing a really great job in safeguarding the nation. I don't know anything about you except your approximate location. Please let me know if I can ever do anything for you," he spoke.

"Sir, if you want to do something for me, please make me meet my father one last time," I said.

Surprised, he said, "I don't understand you."

"You will, Sir," I said and I disconnected the call.

During the festive season, the entire country revelled in joyous celebrations. Recognizing the gravity of the situation, Vijay Chauhan acted with astute understanding and skill. With precise coordinates in hand, he embarked on a covert secret mission. Everything unfolded according to Murtaza's plan, as bombs were successfully planted in the designated buildings. Similarly, the preparations for the attack on India Gate were executed meticulously.

Just an hour before the anticipated blast, Ikhlaq communicated with everyone, confirming that all was in order. The tension mounted as the clock struck eight—the designated time. Ikhlaq, stationed in a hotel, awaited updates on Indian news channels, while we in Pakistan fixated our gaze on television screens—eagerly awaiting news.

However, at precisely eight o'clock, all communication with Ikhlaq and his team abruptly ceased. India experienced a complete blackout, with power and internet shutdowns rendering us unable to establish any contact. Our relentless attempts to reach out to Ikhlaq and the others proved futile.

After approximately 15 minutes, news channels gradually resumed broadcasting. Yet, to our dismay, no mention or coverage of any blast or incident was mentioned. The anticipated news did not materialize, leaving us perplexed and uncertain about the outcome.

Meanwhile, Vijay Chauhan executed a remarkable operation. Tragically, Ikhlaq and the rest of the team were killed in the hotel—their lives were cut short. However, their sinister plans were thwarted as the bombs were successfully defused. Suspects involved in the plot were apprehended, ensuring the nation's integrity and security. Vijay Chauhan's exceptional efforts were vital in averting a devastating catastrophe.

Murtaza remained sleepless, consumed by a profound sense of confusion and despair. His brother and five others were missing, and that uncertainty weighed heavily upon him. He incessantly switched between television channels throughout the night, desperate for any news or information. Countless calls were made, yet no answers were forthcoming.

The long night dragged on, and as the morning light finally broke through, Hafiz made his way to the camp. Lost in deep discussions, our conversation was abruptly interrupted by a sudden flurry of activity. Murtaza's vigilant bodyguards swiftly turned on the television, and to our utter shock, distressing news unfolded before our eyes. It was revealed that six extremists had engaged in a fatal encounter with the army in Kashmir. The magnitude of this revelation was devastating—the six individuals who were reported as deceased were none other than Ikhlaq and his companions who had been dispatched on the mission to Delhi. The weight of this revelation hung thick in the air, leaving us stunned and overwhelmed with grief for the loss of those we had once known.

The failure saddened some, while others grew worried and trembled with apprehension. Although Murtaza appeared calm on the surface, a storm brewed within his eyes. His connection with Ikhlaq ran deep, and it seemed as though he could still feel Ikhlaq's lifeless body in his presence. However, he refrained from exposing himself to that painful sight.

Instead, Murtaza secluded himself in his room for the next five consecutive days. Numerous people, including myself, knocked on his door, seeking a response or any sign of him emerging. Regrettably, he neither replied nor ventured outside. As Friday arrived, the time for prayers beckoned. Murtaza partially opened his door and slid out, proceeding to offer his prayers within the confines of the campground. All of us observed him closely, curious about his actions.

Upon completing his prayers, Murtaza began his journey back to his room. I could not resist intervening because he would lock himself away again. Addressing him, I implored, "How much longer will you confine yourself? Please, find solace and calmness."

"Why do you assume I am upset?" he asked. "My brother, Ikhlaq, has not been killed—he has been martyred. And it is a matter of great pride for me that all three of my brothers have been martyred while serving the purpose of God. No amount of grief can weaken Murtaza Arzai. I sat in solitude, contemplating the price that should be exacted from India for my brother's life. They will undoubtedly have to pay the price, and I will be the one to collect it."

He entered his room, fully opening the door, and revealing a map of India meticulously drawn on the wall with black ink. Multiple Red Cross marks were placed in various locations. Adorned in a black veil from head to toe, he stood before the map. Two individuals hastily brought a video camera and began recording. He was covered entirely—only his eyes were visible. He declared, "My organization takes responsibility for the recent terrorist activity in Kashmir, where the Indian army killed our six brave soldiers. Their sacrifice will not be in vain, and India must pay the price for each of their lives. What occurred in 2008 will be repeated in 2009, but this time, in twelve different locations simultaneously—two blasts in each location as a tribute to the soldiers you have taken from us. Try to stop us if you can."

Another meeting took place at the camp, this time with Hafiz present. However, Murtaza kept the details of the plan to himself, stating that he would personally coordinate everything. He handpicked 12 individuals from the camp, instructing them to travel to various cities in India. He provided them with location points and informed them that they would receive further instructions from his contacts there.

Murtaza expressed his lack of trust in the camp, suspecting that information about their previous mission had been leaked. This revelation surprised everyone in attendance. Hafiz questioned whether anyone was doubted, to which Murtaza replied, "I wonder if I have overlooked something or someone. I don't want to be in doubt this time."

He signalled to his bodyguard and presented a large black bag before the group.

"Please place your mobile phones in this bag," he instructed, as his bodyguard handed the bag to a burning furnace. "This is for the safety of our mission. Be prepared. I will inform you when and how to proceed."

After everyone had left, Murtaza turned to me and said, "I don't doubt you, Shahid, because I consider you a brother. However, for the sake of this mission, I cannot share everything with you either."

The situation was critical, and any mistake could jeopardize everything. I needed to remain vigilant and exhaust all efforts to gather information about his plan.

"Not every instance of silence implies doubt," I reassured Murtaza. "I stand by your side and am ready to sacrifice my life while obeying your commands. I was merely contemplating something. You mentioned that 2008 would be repeated in 2009. You know when it hurts the most? When a wound is repeatedly scratched. So, why not have 26/11 repeat 26/11?"

He was pleased to hear my thoughts and agreed to the idea.

A video recording was circulated widely, creating a significant impact in India. The government and security agencies were on high alert, aware of an imminent threat but unaware of its exact nature. Similarly, I could not contact Suresh due to my damaged phone, making it impossible to give him a hint about the situation and warn Vijay Chauhan. Each passing day grew more stressful and worrisome.

We embarked on our journey to India. The twelve individuals were sent through the *Punj-aab* India-Pakistan Friendship Bus Service, while Murtaza and I travelled via Dubai. On the 24th of November, we arrived in Dubai and after a brief stopover, boarded a private jet to India, which was scheduled to land in the early-morning hours, approximately three and a half hours later.

Chapter 7

The Day: 26ᵗʰ November 2009

We travelled from Dubai to India. As I observed him sitting quietly with his eyes closed, a thought crossed my mind—perhaps ending his life here would bring this story to a close. However, a greater force compelled me to act, for I felt a deep connection to my nation. Despite being an ordinary man, I believed it was my duty to protect India.

"Can I ask you something?" I spoke up, seeking answers.

He responded without opening his eyes, "Of course!"

"What are the benefits of resorting to bomb blasts and shootouts? Why haven't we taken solid and concrete steps to take Kashmir? How long will this game of hide-and-seek continue?"

Confused, he asked, "Why? What do you mean by that? Kashmir has been, is and will always be ours. Let me share something with you. It's not just about Kashmir. It's about our integrity and self-respect. They have always tried to belittle, deceive and ridicule us. They act as if they have done us a favour. This fight will persist until they respect and agree to all our demands. Until then, we will continue to assert our rights and strike where it hurts the most. We will infiltrate their homes, instil fear in their people and make them question each day—they will ask if it is their last. We have brought India to *its* knees multiple times, as we did last year in Mumbai, and will again this year. This atmosphere of fear and panic will force the Indian government to accept our demands."

As he spoke, his words exasperated with anger and hatred.

This conflict will persist indefinitely, and we will ensure that it remains that way. The Indian people will forever dwell in fear and anguish, dependent on our mercy. We hold the power to crush them at our discretion, whenever and wherever we choose. They will be treated like insignificant insects, incapable of inflicting harm upon us. Never will they pose a threat."

As he continued speaking, I carefully observed him, while his bodyguards delighted in his words, wearing smiles on their faces. Curiosity compelled me to inquire about the possibility of them resorting to killings like our own methods.

In response, he erupted into boisterous laughter, applauded and exclaimed, "Those? Kill us? They are cowards, losers—exhausted and helpless. Their only expertise lies in dying, not in killing."

"Allow me to share an anecdote from the Hotel Mumbai attack that occurred last year. Amidst the chaos, I encountered a child, approximately five or six years old, desperately fleeing for his life in the lift lobby. In his panic, he accidentally bumped into me. Engrossed in a phone conversation, likely with his father, the child's father was sobbing and pleading for his survival. My companions suggested leaving the child by recognizing his vulnerability. However, I made the fateful decision and shot him.

What struck me was the child's reaction after being shot. Unfazed by fear, he locked his gaze onto me, exhibiting resolute courage. Rather than fearing death, his greatest concern was being separated from his father. In his final moments, he uttered words, perhaps expressing his love and longing for his father. Observing the unwavering bravery of this young child, he declared, 'My dad will not spare you,' before succumbing to the bomb I detonated."

"He went on to emphasize to me, Shahid, that the incident transcended the age or status of the individuals involved. It revolved around the preservation of fear itself, as he believed that once fear is eradicated, everything is lost."

I questioned what would happen if a seemingly weak person were to exhibit extraordinary courage and seek revenge. In response, he gazed at me intently for a moment, erupted into laughter, and teasingly asked if I was scared.

His laughter was dissolving like poison in my ears, and his voice was ripping my chest. I felt proud of Aditya—for his unwavering faith and love. Today, I learned that he had warned Murtaza about his father's wrath. It was only through his trust and faith in me that we were able to make it this far.

I was consumed by a fiery rage, as every passing moment of Murtaza's existence felt like an unbearable weight upon me. The weight of his life had become insufferable, and I resolved that that day would be the day of his demise. All that remained was to uncover the location of the explosives and orchestrate a torturous end for him.

Despite my persistent efforts, he refrained from divulging explicit details. However, he conveyed a profound statement regarding the historical significance of that special day in India. He proclaimed that the day would be etched in dark ink in the annals of India's history. Anyone who dared to speak of that day and recollect its memories would feel an inexplicable shudder deep down their soul. That day was the chosen day to honour and pay tribute to his brother, Ikhlaq. It would be a day that would epitomize sacrifice and carry profound meaning. His proud proclamation resounded in his words.

The pilot's voice filled the cabin, announcing our arrival in Mumbai. It was imperative to inform Vijay Chauhan immediately, by any means necessary, as he was the sole individual capable of putting an end to all this turmoil. I seized the opportunity, feigning a need to use the restroom, and swiftly made my exit. After pleading desperately and emphasizing the urgency and helplessness of the situation, a sympathetic housekeeping staff member handed me their phone. Without possessing Vijay Chauhan's contact number, I dialled Suresh's number and informed him that something significant was being planned that day. I requested him to connect me with Vijay Chauhan—my heart was racing along with my nerves. Suresh, acting without deliberation, connected the call.

In a voice laced with apprehension, I conveyed to Vijay Chauhan that it would probably be our final conversation. I warned him that the nation was in grave danger, as there were plans to replicate the events of 2008 in 2009. Not only Mumbai but numerous other cities were targeted, their specifics unknown to me. With a heavy heart, I abruptly ended the call.

Without wasting a moment, I hurried towards Murtaza, ensuring that I did not keep him waiting. As I approached, I noticed a well-dressed individual standing beside him, surrounded by a group of BSF commandos. Cautiously, I made my way to them. "Is it done?" Murtaza inquired. I nodded, confirming.

I was then introduced to a man named Rustam Karaciwala, supposedly one of the most prominent diamond merchants in Zaveri Bazaar. As we exited the airport, we settled into a luxurious black and golden Royal Rolls-Royce, while two other vehicles trailed us. Our speed increased as we departed.

However, something gnawed at the back of my mind—an overwhelming realization struck me. *Oh, no! I had unknowingly placed Suresh in grave danger!* As expected, Vijay Chauhan wasted no time tracing the call. It was evident that his last received call had appeared as an ordinary local call. The housekeeping staff member was swiftly located and apprehended, though their knowledge was limited. A sketch was created based on their description. Suresh, fortunately, remained beyond Vijay Chauhan's grasp. The CCTV footage confirmed the presence of the terrorist, Shahid (myself) and Murtaza at Mumbai airport.

After every five kilometres or so, we kept changing our cars and were entering Mumbai. From Royals Rolls to Maruti 800 cars now, we reached Dharavi, Asia's largest slum. Following Rustam, we passed through the slums and reached a small apartment. There was a stench all around, water logging and narrow streets.

As we entered the room, we found ourselves in a high-tech chamber. Multiple television screens displayed a live feed of various cities under intense surveillance. The footage revealed busy streets, famous landmarks and crowded locations filled with people going about their daily lives. Amidst this visual panorama, a group of six to seven alert bodyguards stood in a room, their attention fixed on the screens before them. They all greeted Murtaza warmly.

Murtaza instructed Rustam to provide a briefing on the arrangements, but before he could begin, his phone rang. He smiled and asked one of the bodyguards to switch on the news channel. An advisory was being announced on the news channels, displaying Murtaza's and my photos, urging anyone who had seen us to report the information. Additionally, everyone was advised to stay at home as the city was under threat.

Both Rustam and Murtaza burst into laughter, remarking that it was their *home* which was in danger that day, yet everyone was being asked to stay there. Interrupting their laughter, I asked, "What's next? You used to say, 'Why don't we attack from the front?' Let's do the same. This Vijay Chauhan is very fond of becoming a hero. Let's see what he can do today."

Murtaza dialled Vijay Chauhan's number on a satellite phone, and as he answered, Murtaza introduced himself confidently. "Vijay Chauhan, I'm sure you've heard my name. No matter how hard you try, you will not be able to stop me again today. This is not about India. It is now more about you and me. I know you killed my dear brother, Ikhlaq. He was dearest to me, and because of you, I couldn't even see him one last time. He couldn't even have a proper burial. Today, I stand alone," he spoke with conviction.

"What will you achieve by being alone?" Vijay Chauhan retorted. "Let me kill you as well. You're in Mumbai, right? I will bury you in the hole where you're hiding." Vijay Chauhan threatened.

Murtaza smiled and responded, "Only when you can find me. Don't waste your time tracing this call. Instead, make sure people stay in their homes and mind you, it's important. One last piece of advice—ensure that your family also stays at home."

He laughed and disconnected the call.

Finally, his plan was revealed. Murtaza instructed Rustam to disclose the final plan. I was given the responsibility of carrying out the bombings in 12 cities including 7 metro cities, including Mumbai and of course the Taj Hotel for a 26/11 repeat. Since Rustam was a prominent gold merchant with an elite clientele, the plan involved targeting influential individuals such as actors, businessmen, politicians, internationally recognized artists, diplomats and sports celebrities.

Murtaza instructed Rustam to prepare a list of his high-profile customers from the above category, who had recently purchased jewellery from him, and their deliveries were scheduled for that day at their home. There were 48 such people, and each delivery was intended to include a powerful bomb alongside the jewellery. A special gift was scheduled to be delivered to Vijay Chauhan's house as well. The unsuspecting delivery boys had no knowledge of this deadly payload. They were given a common delivery time, and their phones were connected to a shared call that Murtaza was going to make to all of them simultaneously. They were informed that a delivery code would be required upon reaching their respective destinations, and the customer would accept the package only after providing the code. The plan was carefully designed so that when Murtaza received each of their calls in one go, the explosions would occur, resulting in significant casualties.

Murtaza also arranged to go live on all news channels after the bombings to proclaim to the world that he had accomplished what he had promised. We had 12 cities and 48 locations displayed on the screens, where those packages were scheduled to be delivered. Everyone watched the screens intently, as within the next 15 minutes, all the packages were expected to reach their destinations. Murtaza eagerly awaited his success—his cunning smile clearly visible on his face.

It was time to get over all that. I was not liking his being alive anymore. I could not tolerate his presence any longer. Stepping back, I aimed my firearm at Rustam's head with unwavering determination, and with a single, fatal shot, his life ended abruptly.

Before Murtaza could fully comprehend the unfolding events, I swiftly shifted my aim towards him. My gun fired, striking both his knees mercilessly. The excruciating pain ripped through his body, causing him to collapse onto the ground.

As the tension in the room escalated, bodyguards lunged at me with swift and calculated movements. The air crackled with anticipation as the fight unfolded. I prepared for the assault and demonstrated remarkable agility and skill.

The first bodyguard lunged forward and launched a powerful punch. However, I expertly dodged the attack, swiftly countering it with a precise kick that sent the bodyguard crashing into a nearby wall, incapacitated.

Without missing a beat, another bodyguard charged, attempting a series of rapid strikes. But I effortlessly evaded each blow, thus showcasing lightning-fast reflexes. With a swift manoeuvre, I disarmed my opponent, using the guard's weapon against him, thus rendering him defenceless with a decisive blow.

Undeterred by their fallen comrades, the remaining bodyguards intensified their assault. They attacked from different angles, their movements synchronized and ruthless. But I remained composed, while I utilized a combination of evasive manoeuvres and calculated strikes.

In a whirlwind of actions, I delivered a flurry of devastating blows, which swiftly neutralized each bodyguard—one by one. But I was hit badly too. One had stuck a long knife in my waist from behind.

In the room, only Murtaza and I remained alive. He writhed in agony, his voice filled with disbelief as he mustered the strength to ask, "Why, Shahid?"

The sound of his voice disgusted me and fuelled my anger even further. Without hesitation, I grabbed a knife and unleashed a relentless onslaught of strikes upon his body. With each blow, the room seemed to echo with his agonizing screams.

Amidst the brutality, Murtaza's phone began ringing—most likely the delivery boys had reached their destinations. Enraged, I grabbed the phone and violently smashed it against the ground, thus shattering it into countless pieces. The danger had passed, and Murtaza's mission had failed, but my mission was far from over. Blood seeped from his wounds, as there was no place left untouched by my vicious assault. However, I purposely avoided striking his neck, denying him the mercy of a swift death. This was *my promise to my father* and *my pursuit of justice for Aditya.*

Moaning in pain, Murtaza crawled towards me and uttered, "I treated you like my brother, and you did this to me?"

Disgust coursed through my veins as I responded, "I never knew you. I had a happy life with my wife and child. But in a single moment, you shattered my world. Everything was taken away. And do you know what today is? It's my son's birthday—26th November. And do you know when he died? It was the same day—26th November. He was waiting for me to celebrate his birthday but I couldn't. Do you know why? Because you killed him," I declared with a mix of sorrow and fury.

Murtaza, bewildered and shocked, muttered, "I killed him?"

I knelt, bringing my face close to his ear, and whispered, "Mumbai, 26th November 2008. 'Miss You, Dad.'"

The realization dawned upon him, and his eyes widened in horror.

"That child had said rightly—his father did come and will not leave you. I am his father, *Avinash*, and he was my son *Aditya*!"

Time was running out for both of us. I decided to make one final call to my father using the satellite phone.

Unbeknown to Suresh, who was being apprehended, the call was being tracked. It took a skilled and perfect hacker like Suresh to accomplish such a feat. The location was traced, and Vijay Chauhan issued orders to his people to reach the location and eliminate the target without hesitation or questions. Suresh remained oblivious to the fact that I was the one making the call until he heard my voice as I spoke to my father.

"Dad, it's time to go. Let your son go now, as his son is waiting for him. I tried my best to fulfil my duty as much as I understood it. If I missed anything, please forgive me. Today, the promise I made to you has been fulfilled. Only one task remains, and I must end this call as time slips away," I whispered tearfully.

The mark of a terrorist stained my existence, and I could not depart without cleansing it. Otherwise, society would not grant my father and Sonali the dignity that they deserved. I switched on the camera and positioned it in front of Murtaza, capturing the scene live on air. I began speaking, not to justify my actions or present myself not as a criminal or terrorist, nor to find a way to pay homage to my son, Aditya. I only wanted Dad and Sonali not to be known as the family of a terrorist. As I continued sharing my story, the sound of approaching police sirens grew louder.

Suresh attempted to intervene, urging Vijay Chauhan to save me, but it was too late. The police arrived, breaking down the door, and a barrage of indiscriminate gunfire erupted.

In my last fleeting moments, I whispered through tears, "Miss you, Dad."

The End

The actions of Avinash were truly remarkable and displayed immense bravery—something that no one had ever thought to be possible. His intent to carry out such a daring act was beyond the imagination of many and was not something that most people would ever attempt.

The video that went viral on the day of Murtaza Arzai's execution was a powerful testament to Avinash's courage. Although the camera broke during the fire and no one could see it completely, Vijay Chauhan managed to see it, which dispelled all doubts that he had about Avinash's character. Previously, Vijay had always considered him to be one of the criminals but the video changed his perspective.

Through the video, Vijay realized that Avinash was not an enemy but a grieving father seeking revenge for his son. The footage showcased Avinash's bravery and determination as he risked his life to avenge his son's death. It was a poignant reminder of the powerful emotions that drive people to take drastic actions in the face of tragedy.

Astonishingly, a regular man could go to great lengths alone, breaching all the roadblocks. Vijay deeply regretted his misunderstanding of Avinash and his order for his men to open fire against him. He did his best to save him as he learned about his truth just after his orders, and probably that was too late. All his anger and hatred for Avinash had now turned into respect, sympathy and sorrow. He had learned that he was not a terrorist but a brave father.

Sadly, Avinash was gone, and his body was lying unattended in one of the corners of a crematorium under the custody of the local police.

Vijay Chauhan arrived at the crematorium angrily, demanding to know why Avinash's body was lying on the floor. A policeman replied callously, saying that Avinash was a terrorist and deserved to be treated as such. But Vijay knew the truth—Avinash was not a terrorist and deserved to be honoured.

After much effort and negotiation, Vijay finally obtained possession of Avinash's body, and his video was played on a national news channel with sensitivity and respect for the content. The video had a powerful impact on the people who showed their respect and admiration for Avinash. This also proved that he was not a terrorist but an ordinary man—a father with no other choice.

It was Avinash's last journey to Banaras and his house. Vijay arrived early in the morning, just before sunrise, with Avinash's body. When he knocked on the door, an old trembling voice asked, "Who is there?"

Vijay replied, "Your son has come to see you, Mr. Tripati. Please open the door. It's Avinash." The door opened, and Avinash's father saw a policeman standing before him with teary eyes.

Smiling, he replied, "So he's finally home. I was waiting only for him. Just give me five minutes."

Avinash's father went inside, leaving Vijay standing at the door.

He began to wash the courtyard with water and mop it properly. Vijay watched him from the door. "Can you please bring him inside now?" Avinash's father asked Vijay.

Many people gathered around the house. Vijay and the other policemen carried Avinash's body into the courtyard, where it was gently and respectfully laid on the floor.

Sonali placed a burning clay lamp near his head and sat down. "Can you unwrap his face?" she asked Vijay. He signalled to a policeman, who did the needful. Avinash's father brought a few pictures and held them tightly to his chest. He placed them near Avinash's head. They were pictures of Aditi, Aditya, Prakash and his mother.

Sitting on his knees, and lovingly stroking Avinash's forehead, he said, "You are tired and now you must leave. They are all waiting for you. I wish I could come along, but I still have the responsibility of looking after Sonali and the kids. I will see you soon, my son."

He had a smile on his face and pride in his eyes.

He looked at Vijay and said, "Thank you. Avinash told me you would bring him to me. I hope he fought well and was tough to handle."

Vijay nodded and said, "In my entire career, till now, I never witnessed such bravery in a person like your son. I am sorry I could not save him. I found out about the truth when it was too late."

He bowed down to Avinash with folded hands and asked permission to take him for his last rites.

"I have one request. My people and I will take Avinash for the last rites. I don't want you to bear this burden once again," Vijay said while pleading with folded hands.

Avinash's father nodded and said, "Yes, now I don't have that much strength left. I have become old, a little weak and my vision has faded too."

Avinash began his last journey. Being a son of his father and being a father to his son, he did all that he could do.

Bidding a final goodbye, his father solemnly lit his funeral pyre. Avinash set out on his last journey to reach his destination—where he could reunite with Aditya and Aditi and experience eternal happiness.

"Love is a wondrous force that transcends physical presence. It carves a unique space in our hearts where we cherish those whom we love, whether they are near or far. In that sacred place, we hold onto them and carry their essence with us for eternity, creating an everlasting bond that is endured through time."

Avinash met Aditi and Aditya in a place where he could look proudly into their eyes with no guilt and pain. It was a place where they could live together for infinity.

It was a serene morning with the melodious chirping of birds that were flying over the sparkling sea. The chirping was like a symphony—belonging to Nature's music. The rhythmic clinking of the waves resonated in the air, accompanied by the gentle caress of the cool breeze, which felt like a blessing from heaven. Aditya was engrossed in building an intricate sandcastle on the shore with his imagination taking him to his world. Avinash and Aditi watched him with contentment, while they sat on a sturdy rock, holding hands and enjoying the blissful atmosphere.

Suddenly, Avinash interrupted Aditya's playtime and said, "Come on, Aditya, let's head back to the hotel and grab breakfast. Today is your birthday, and we must prepare for the evening party too."

His words broke the peaceful silence, but Aditya's eyes lit up excitedly when he realized that it was his special day.

They strolled back to the hotel—*The Hotel Taj*. They stood staring at it and were standing across the Gateway of India!

Verse 1:

I'm a traveller of the setting night;

I left behind a world without light.

I couldn't stay;

My soul took a flight to pay my debt,

To make things right.

Chorus:

I could not live with you,

But I paid your rights after death.

Your happiness in my heart, it's true,

I'll search for you in heaven with each breath.

Verse 2:

I took your memories with me,

As I journeyed towards eternity.

I hope one day you'll forgive me,

For the pain, I caused, for my vanity.

Chorus:

I could not live with you,

But I paid your rights after the death.

Your happiness, in my heart, it's true;

I'll search for you in heaven with each breath.

Bridge:

I'll keep looking for you, my love,

In every star and dove.

I'll keep searching until we meet,

In heaven's embrace; so bittersweet.

Chorus:

I could not live with you,

But I paid your rights after death.

Your happiness in my heart, it's true;

I'll search for you in heaven with each breath.

Outro:

I'm a traveller of the setting night;

I'll keep searching for you, my light.

In heaven's embrace, we'll reunite and shine so bright together.